Please return/renew this item by the
last date shown to avoid a charge.
Books may also be renewed by phone
and Internet. May not be renewed if
required by another reader.

www.libraries.barnet.gov.uk

BARNET
LONDON BOROUGH

Bookwitch

ALSO BY SALLY NICHOLLS

SALLY

An Island
of Our
Own

NICHOLLS

■SCHOLASTIC

First published in the UK in 2015 by Scholastic Children's Books
An imprint of Scholastic Ltd
Euston House, 24 Eversholt Street,
London, NW1 1DB, UK
Registered office: Westfield Road, Southam, Warwickshire, CV47 0RA
SCHOLASTIC and associated logos are trademarks and/or registered
trademarks of Scholastic Inc.

ISBN 978 1407 12433 9

A CIP catalogue record for this book is available from the British Library.

Printed and bound by CPI Group (UK) Ltd, Croydon, CR0 4YY
Papers used by Scholastic Children's Books are made from
wood grown in sustainable forests.

1 3 5 7 9 10 8 6 4 2

www.scholastic.co.uk

*A lot is written about people who are wrong
or obnoxious or cruel on the internet.
This book is dedicated to all the people who are kind and generous.
And particularly all the people who are kind and generous to me.
Thank you.*

I don't have a staffroom, but if I did, you'd be in it.

No man is an island entire of itself; every man is a piece of the continent, a part of the main.

JOHN DONNE

AN ISLAND OF OUR OWN

I told my brother Jonathan I was going to write a book about all the things that happened to us last year. About the home-made spaceships, and the lock-pickers, and the thermal lances, and the exploding dishwasher, and the island that was old when the Vikings came, and Auntie Irene's treasure, and all the things that happened before we found it.

"It's going to be brilliant!" I told him. "I've already got a title. *An Island of Our Own*! Isn't it great?"

"But we don't have an island of our own," said Jonathan. "People are going to pick it up and expect it to be *Swallows and Amazons* for rich people! And then they'll read it and there'll be no island and they'll hate you! They'll put grenades through your window!"

I told Jonathan people didn't put grenades through your window just because of what you called your book.

But Jonathan said you shouldn't underestimate the rage of a fandom. "Look at *Star Wars* fans," he said. "I would totally put a grenade through George Lucas's window if I thought it would get him to take Jar Jar Binks out of *The Phantom Menace*." Which seems a little harsh given how much Jonathan loves *Star Wars*, but Jonathan said you should never expect logic from a fanatic. Which is probably true.

So I said I'd tell people at the beginning of the book that the title wasn't about a real island, but a metaphorical one (although there *is* a real island in the story – several, in fact), and also not to put grenades through my window, but send cake instead.

"There," I said. "Satisfied? Can I start now?"

THINGS YOU NEED
TO KNOW ABOUT ME

Here are the things you need to know about me. My name is Holly Theresa Kennet. I have never written a book before, which is hardly surprising, because I'm only thirteen, but I've read a lot of books, so I know that you start by introducing your characters. Like, if this was a Sherlock Holmes story, it would start with people knocking on Sherlock Holmes's door, and then Holmes would take one look at them and tell you that she's a left-handed seamstress who plays the flute and likes pickled onions, and he's a retired insomniac army colonel with a pet hamster.

I have tried doing this on people, but it's a lot harder in real life. Like, I've got a photo here beside me of me and my school friends, which was taken last year, just before this story starts. (I look different now. I'm growing my

3

hair, for one thing.) What can you deduce about me from this picture? Well, you can tell I'm about twelve, and you can see that I go to St Augustine's Academy, because I'm wearing a hideous school uniform that makes me look like a plum, and you can see I probably don't much care about how I look, because I've got this shaggy-dog sort of haircut, which is falling in my eyes because it's been ages since I got it cut, and also because I'm not wearing any make-up, unlike Sufiya and Kali, who are wearing not just make-up but nail extensions, and earrings, and hairspray, and all sorts of stuff which is technically banned in our school, but nobody cares.

You can also see that Issy and I are the only white kids in the photo, which I guess tells you something about where we live. It's a little flat over a chip shop in this part of London which is famous for being – I dunno – fabulously diverse and cultural and having lots of great food shops or something. It *does* have lots of great food shops. You can buy all sorts of wonderful things at the grocers' round here, like baklava, and pomegranates, and sharon fruit, and sticky Indian sweets, and great big bags of rice dead cheap. And there are shops that sell saris in hundreds of different colours, and shops that only sell Polish food, and coffee shops with Turkish hookah pipes and lots of stuff like that.

When I was little I used to love this series of books called *The Chalet School*, about a school in the Alps where all the kids came from different countries and spoke different languages and instead of doing PE you went and climbed mountains, and someone was always wandering off on their own and falling off a cliff. Our school isn't in the Alps, and our PE lessons are dead boring, but it *is* a bit like *The Chalet School* in that everyone comes from all over the world, and not just boring countries like Switzerland, but India, and Pakistan, and Bangladesh, and Kenya, and Ethiopia, and loads of really cool places that I'm totally going to visit one day when I'm an environmental scientist, or possibly an environmental campaigner for Greenpeace, I haven't decided yet. I will have to travel there by boat, because I'm against aeroplanes, because they give off too much carbon, but I could totally get to Africa on a boat. People used to do it all the time in Victorian days. My friend Sizwe says I can stay with his aunt and uncle in South Africa, and my other friend Neema says I can stay with her gran in Pakistan, so I wouldn't even have to pay for hotels or anything.

Anyway. What you can also see in the photo is that my school bag is held together with gaffer tape. And my winter coat is a bit small and doesn't *quite* do up. What you *can't* see is that my shoes are slightly too tight, and pinch at the toes. Or that my school shirt used to belong to my brother, Jonathan, who is seven years older than me, and is way too big. I mean, Sherlock Holmes could probably see that, but you can't really in this picture because I'm wearing a blazer on top.

Sherlock Holmes might think that my too-small shoes and my too-big shirt meant that my mum didn't care about me, but actually I don't have a mum. She died when I was eleven. And I don't have a dad either. He died when I was six. I am a real, genuine orphan. There are lots of orphans in books, but I'm the only one I know in real life apart from my big brother, Jonathan, and my little brother, Davy, who's seven.

Davy and I live with Jonathan. He's our legal guardian. This is kind of weird, because he was only eighteen when my mum died, and still basically a kid.

When I tell kids at school that I live with my brother, they always ask loads of questions. Some of them are really stupid, like "Did your parents die in a car crash?" ("No. Why does everyone think that? My mum didn't even have a car.") Sometimes they just go all over the top feeling sorry for me, like, "Oh my God, both your parents are dead! That's so sad! I can't even imagine what that would be like!" This is mostly annoying, because they usually want you to comfort them. Which is *really* stupid, because *I'm* the one with the dead parents.

The question people ask most often is "What's it like?" And the answer to that one is complicated.

This book is partly about what it's like being kids who raise ourselves and partly about all the things that happened to us last summer. I don't think even Sherlock Holmes would be able to guess the things that happened to us. I'm not sure I even *believe* they happened, sometimes.

But they did.

CATH'S CAFF

Because my mum is dead, Jonathan has to earn enough money to look after us. Fortunately, he already had a job when Mum died. He worked in Cath's Caff, running the till while Cath fried bacon and sausages in the kitchen, and making coffee in the big coffee machine, and clearing tables, and loading the big dishwasher, and mopping the floor at the end of the day.

The job was just supposed to be for the summer, though. Jonathan is dead clever. He was supposed to go to university in September, to study maths and physics.

He had to cancel his university place when Mum died. He pretends he doesn't mind, but I bet he does. I would, if I was him. Now he just works in the café all day, and looks after us in the evenings.

Cath's Caff opens at seven a.m., so we all get up

dead early in the mornings. When Mum first died, Jonathan was always late for work, because he is rubbish at mornings, and he is even more rubbish at mornings when he has to get Davy and me up and dressed and find the stuff we need for school and all that sort of thing. He still isn't as good at it as Mum was. It's been a year and a half since anyone shined my shoes, for example, and we're always forgetting important bits of homework, and non-uniform days, and swimming costumes, and money for bake sales. But at least we usually get to the café by sevenish now.

When we get to the café, Jonathan has to start work making people coffees and taking breakfast orders. Cath makes me and Davy breakfast while we wait. We have bacon sandwiches with lots of ketchup and big mugs of milky tea. It's my job to make sure Davy doesn't get ketchup down his school jumper, and to make sure his hair is brushed and his shoelaces tied and all that stuff. Then, at a quarter past eight, I walk him to school and get the bus to St Augustine's. That bit was easier when we both went to the same school, but as long as the bus isn't too late, I'm usually OK.

Jonathan doesn't finish work until half past four, so I have to make sure I'm on the first bus out of school, or I'm late for Davy. Davy's school *does* have an after-school club, and he's technically a member, but they charge you more for every extra fifteen minutes you stay there, so I'm not allowed to talk to my mates after school, or go and buy sweets from the corner shop, or anything like that. I have to go and get Davy quick.

When people say, "So your brother looks after you?" I usually say, "Actually, Jonathan looks after me, and Jonathan and me look after Davy." I am just as much a parent as Jonathan is, even though I'm only a kid. When Mum first died, I was allowed to look after myself, but Davy had to go to the after-school club. I didn't mind. My friend Sizwe looked after himself too, because his mum runs this cleaning firm and he doesn't have a dad, so we used to hang out together, which was fun. But when I turned twelve, Jonathan said I was old enough to look after Davy. Also, after-school club was expensive and we needed the money.

See, the thing with Jonathan is, he doesn't make quite enough money to pay for everything. He makes enough money to pay the rent and buy food, and usually there's a little bit left over. But the problem is, then Davy gets invited to a birthday party and needs to buy a birthday present. Or it's Christmas. Or the washing machine breaks. Or my shoes get too small. Or there's a school trip. And at first, we just used to spend the money in the bank, because birthday parties and new shoes and washing machines are important. But then we spent all Mum's savings and didn't have any money left. And then we went into negative money. And then we started to panic.

So now I keep Davy entertained until Jonathan finishes work. Sometimes we go Cath's Caff and wait for him to finish, but it's a bit boring, and Cath only gives us free food if there are stale doughnuts waiting to be thrown out or something like that, and there aren't usually.

Davy is pretty easy to look after, though. For someone who's only seven, he's very easy, actually. I mean, I just have to make him a sandwich, and he's quite happy to build things with his Lego or play with his rabbit, Sebastian, who is a house rabbit and very tame, because we don't have a garden. I don't really *mind*. Most of the time. Most of the time I think it's quite cool, like I'm a Young Carer or a Teen Mum or something. Nearly Teen. Nearly Teen Surrogate Mum.

It's only sometimes, when my friends are all going off to do something without me, that I care. Sometimes it would be nice to go and hang out with Neema and Sizwe at the park, and not have to hurry off to pick up Davy.

GRANDPARENTS

Every Wednesday, Davy and I go and stay with my gran and grandad for the night. We started doing it after my mum died, when I was only eleven. Now I'm older, and don't really need looking after any more, but I still go. I like my grandparents.

Gran and Grandad live in this teeny tiny flat in one of those buildings that aren't quite an old people's home, but have buttons you can press if you fall over and need help, and people who come and check on you if they haven't seen you for a couple of days and stuff like that. Gran and Grandad are pretty old. Gran is seventy-nine, and Grandad is eighty-seven. Grandad had a stroke a couple of years ago, so he doesn't really talk, and half of his face is all mushed-up-looking. He can only really use one side of his body, and he has to sit in a wheelchair.

That's why we don't live with them, because Gran has her hands full looking after Grandad, and also he wouldn't be able to live in our flat because the door is too narrow for his wheelchair, and he wouldn't be able to get up the stairs.

Just because Grandad can't really talk, it doesn't mean he's stupid. He's not. He's just as smart as he always was. You just have to take a bit longer to work out what he's trying to say, that's all.

I like going to Gran and Grandad's flat, because everything there is just the same as it always used to be. There's the same shelf of children's books that used to belong to my mum and my auntie. Davy has the same box of toys to play with that I used to have when I was little. I can sit and read a book, or watch telly, or do my homework, or whatever, and the flat is always warm, even in winter. And Gran cooks dinner – proper dinner, with vegetables and meat – and we play games.

We've always played games with Gran and Grandad. We play whist, and Cheat, and Bloody Mary, and Hungarian drinking games, with Davy on the same team as Grandad, because he always forgets the rules. When I'm feeling sad, I sometimes wish I could live here, in a tidy house with proper food every night. I can't, though. I know I can't. So mostly, I try not to worry about it.

REVIEWING THE SITUATION

The other thing that happens is reviews from social services. Reviews happen twice a year, which is the only time our flat ever gets cleaned.

We all help. Jonathan washes up, I dry, and Davy puts away. I make piles of all our mess, which Davy takes upstairs and dumps in the bottom of our wardrobes. We throw away all the rubbish which usually lives on every flat surface. (I'm in charge of taking things out of the rubbish and putting them in the recycling. Jonathan's in charge of taking unpaid bills and letters from school out of the recycling and putting them in the bottom of his wardrobe.) Davy likes to hoover. We tried to persuade him that housework was fun, and he should do all our housework for us, all the time, but it didn't work.

Jonathan is in charge of the details. He goes round and wipes the coffee drips off the kitchen cabinets, and dusts the mantelpiece, and windowsills, and cleans the bathroom.

A review is what you're supposed to have every six months if you're in foster care, which Davy and I are technically are, even though we just live with our brother in the same flat we always did. This way Jonathan is technically a foster carer, so he gets money from the government for looking after us. I wasn't sure I wanted to be in care at first, because I thought it meant that social workers could come and take us away if they thought Jonathan wasn't doing a good enough job. But it turns out that social workers don't actually like taking kids away, and we need the money. And also this way we have someone to ring up if we need help.

Lots of people come to a review. There's me and Davy and Jonathan, and my and Davy's social worker, who is called Abigail, and Jonathan's social worker, who is called Philip, and the person in charge of the review, who is called Sheila.

We're also supposed to have someone come from school. This is easy for Davy, who just has his classroom teacher. It's a bit more complicated for me, now I'm in secondary school. The first review after I started at St Augustine's, I had my form tutor come. The second time, the time before our story starts, I had my head of year, Mr Matthews. Mr Matthews was all right. I didn't really know him. He was the person who came out of his office and told us all to shut up when we were messing about at lunchtimes, and who handed out merit certificates when you got ten stickers in your planner, which was even less of a big deal than it sounds. It was *seriously* weird seeing him there in our living room. I don't even have my school friends round to our flat, mostly because it's too embarrassing trying to explain why it's always a mess.

Davy had his review first, and I had to wait upstairs while that was happening. Davy's review would be fine, I knew. Davy is the sort of little kid everyone likes. I was a bit worried about his homework, because we don't always manage to make sure that gets done. He usually finishes his worksheets and things, because he hates being told off, so he worries until he's done them, and it's not like you have to force him to sit down and work or anything. But things like spelling and tables, where you just have to learn things, we often don't bother with.

Davy's review didn't take that long. I sat upstairs and read my book. I like books a lot. At the moment, I'm mostly reading books about detectives, or about the end of the world. I love Sherlock Holmes and Agatha Christie, and I don't even mind that they're grown-up books. I'm only twelve when this story starts, but I read lots of grown-up books. Most of the grown-up books I read aren't much more difficult or scary than books for people my age. I mean, even Agatha Christie never kills twenty-two kids in one book, like they do in *The Hunger Games*.

After what felt like ages but really wasn't that long, I heard Davy's feet tramping up the stairs to my room. Our flat is half of an old Victorian house that once had four storeys. The bottom storey is Ranjit's fish and chip shop. Then there's the living room and the kitchen. Then Davy's room (which he used to share with Jonathan but doesn't any more because now Jonathan sleeps in my mum's old room) and the bathroom. Jonathan and I sleep right in the roof, in the rooms that used to belong to servants. My room is little, with a slopey roof and a skylight and a dormer window that sticks out of the roof. When I lie in bed at night, I can hear the rain battering down right above my head, and the goods trains rattling through the night. I love it.

"Your turn," said Davy, coming through into my room. He looked very small and sweet.

"Did it go OK?" I asked.

He shrugged. "Mrs Henderson brought all my pictures," he said. "And my topic book, and my maths book. And they asked if I wanted anything to be different, and I said I didn't."

All the grown-ups were sitting in the living room when I went down. Our living room isn't that big, so they were mostly sitting on kitchen chairs. Mrs Henderson was just leaving. She knows me from picking Davy up from school.

"Hello, Holly," she said, smiling at me. "How's it going?"

"Good," I said. "Brilliant, actually. Nothing to worry about."

I didn't say that to the other grown-ups, though. It's stupid to not have enough money to buy things like new shoes, when the state is supposed to be looking after you. And I was going to tell them so.

"We need more money," I said.

The social workers exchanged glances.

Jonathan said, "*Holly*. Don't be rude." Like normally he makes me be so polite!

"What?" I said. "We do. We were all right before," I explained, looking directly at the two social workers, "because we had Mum's savings. But we've spent them. And now there's loads of stuff I need. School shoes, and a school bag, and our form's supposed to be going to Alton Towers at the end of term, and we need money for that." I gave them a stern look.

Jonathan's social worker, Philip-the-dull, said, "Is this true, Jonathan?"

"Well." Jonathan looked embarrassed. "Well. Yes. I was going to talk to you about it, actually. There are some things we need, and we don't really have the money to pay for them."

"And foster kids aren't supposed to be *starving*, are we?" I burst in. "I mean, not that we're starving, but, you know. We should have school bags, shouldn't we?"

"Yes, you should," said my social worker, Abigail. She leant forward. "I was going to talk to Jonathan about this, actually. The thing is, Holly, there are two levels of foster-care allowance. Jonathan's on the lower level, because he's a family member, you understand? But if you really can't cope on the lower level, we can see about getting you transferred to the higher level. We talked about it at the last review, didn't we?"

"Yes," said Jonathan. He looked – I'm not sure, exactly. Awkward. Ashamed? "I do try," he said. "It's just when . . . things happen unexpectedly. They tip us up."

"That's life, I'm afraid," said Philip-the-dull. He made a note in his book. "OK. I'm not promising anything, but I think we can probably swing it. I'm not sure how long it'll take, though, so don't buy anything expensive for the next couple of months, OK?"

"But I'm sure we'll be able to get some money released for Alton Towers, Holly," said Abigail, smiling at me.

"And school shoes," said Jonathan. "Holly's got a whacking great hole in the sole, haven't you, Holl."

"Of course," said Abigail. She made another note. "Shall we talk about your school work now, Holly?"

I gave an *enormous* groan. "It's *mostly* OK," I said. By which I meant, the subjects I like are OK. "You know," I said hopefully, "I read about this scheme where kids got paid money to go to school. We couldn't do that, could we?"

"Hmm," said Abigail. "No. We couldn't."

WEIRD THINGS ABOUT BEING
PRETEND GROWN-UPS

I know really that I'm a kid and Jonathan's in charge of me, but it's not that simple because I do just as much washing-up as he does, and also because when there are difficult decisions to be made, I at least get a *say* in what we do. If Mum was a proper grown-up, and Jonathan is maybe three-quarters grown-up, then I'm at least a quarter grown-up. Maybe even a half.

Like, take the thing that happened the Friday after the review. Gran rang to say that Mum's Auntie Irene had had a stroke and was very ill in hospital, and could we go and visit her on Saturday, because Gran didn't have anyone to leave Grandad with. I wanted to say no, because it's our Saturday, and we can do what we want with our own Saturday, and isn't that the best part about not having our lives run by grown-ups? And also because

I like Auntie Irene, and I don't like hospitals, and I didn't really want to have to go and see what Auntie Irene looked like in one if I didn't have to. I like happy things, not sad ones.

"Let's not," I said to Jonathan. "It'll just be weird, and she probably won't even know we're there, and . . . it's not like we see her that much when she's *well*. Why should we suddenly go and see her now?"

But Jonathan said part of being a pretend grown-up is actually doing the grown-up bits, otherwise we're just kids, and if we're just kids then this whole thing falls apart. And also he wanted to see Auntie Irene, because he liked Auntie Irene, and if Mum was here, she'd go. Which is true. She would. Keeping in touch with relations was one of the things Mum was good at and me and Jonathan are bad at. We still get loads of Christmas cards at Christmas, and we never send any back. Well, Davy and I send ones to the kids at school, but that's it. I feel bad about that, and also like there's this important part of being a grown-up that we're missing. So then I decided that Jonathan was right, and going to see Auntie Irene was absolutely what we ought to do.

Even though I didn't really want to.

AUNTIE IRENE'S STORY

This is who Auntie Irene was.

Auntie Irene was little and fierce, like my mum. She was also really, really smart. When they were kids, Grandad went to the school at the end of the road and left at fourteen. But Auntie Irene won a scholarship to grammar school. And then she went to university, and studied Further Advanced Engineering For Really Brainy People. Or something like that, anyway.

And then . . . well, I'm not exactly sure what happened next, but it ended up with her getting a job designing machines in a big designing-machines factory. (Probably. That's totally a thing, right?) And then she left the designing-machines place and set up her own company as *an inventor*. I *know*! A real, genuine inventor! I've seen photographs, and basically it was a big laboratory thing, where Auntie Irene and lots of her engineer buddies sat around with drawing boards and machines and invented stuff.

Auntie Irene said it wasn't really like that. She said mostly they worked to commission – people would call them up and say, "Can you design us a super-fast bicycle to send to the Olympics?" Or a new type of safety belt. Or whatever. And then they'd do it. She said sometimes it was a lot of fun, and sometimes it was boring, but what it usually was was "profitable".

Auntie Irene had lots of money. I'm not sure how much, because I never asked, but lots. She had a lovely big house in the country with a swimming pool, and an orchard with lots of apple trees, and she used to have a yacht when she was young, but she sold it when she got old.

"Never get old, kiddos," she used to say to us. "Getting old is the pits."

Auntie Irene liked us, I think. She liked my mum, anyway. She used to do things with my mum when she came to London, which was quite a lot. When I was little, she did things with me and Jonathan too. She took us to see *The Phantom of the Opera* when I was six, and she used to sit and have long, tech-y conversations with Jonathan about telescopes, and electrons, and computers. She was my favourite relation after Gran and Grandad.

Mostly, Auntie Irene was cool, but not everyone thought so. Grandad thought she was difficult and shouty. If she ever disagreed with you about anything, she'd spend ages and ages telling you why you were wrong, even if you were six, and what you were saying was "Ariel is cooler than Mulan." Also, she used to sweep in and be wonderful for an evening, and then disappear for months and months and never answer her phone and just forget to come to people's weddings.

She and her husband had one daughter, whose name is Jo, but they didn't get on. I can sort of see why. Auntie Irene was pretty controlling, and she was apparently always nagging Jo and saying she wasn't doing enough with her life or working hard enough at whatever she was doing. And whatever Jo did, Auntie Irene always wanted her to do it better. I like Jo, though. I'd like to see more of her, but she's always pretty busy. She lives on the other side of London, and she runs a catering company with her husband, and she has two little boys, who are called Noah and Alfie and are very cute. She used to keep sending us birthday and Christmas cards that said things like *We MUST meet up soon*, but we never did.

Auntie Irene was married to Uncle Evan. No one likes Uncle Evan. I mean, *no one*. Uncle Evan is horrible. Even when we *did* see Auntie Irene, I hardly ever saw Uncle Evan – because Auntie Irene used to come to London on her own – but whenever I did, he used to just sit there and grump and complain.

"Why do you put up with him, Irene?" Gran said to her once. That was pretty brave of Gran. Mostly, people didn't argue with Auntie Irene.

But Auntie Irene just scrunched her mouth up. "Oh,

well . . ." she said. "There aren't many people can put up with me. It's nice not to be the bad guy all the time."

I know Auntie Irene didn't trust him, though. Auntie Irene didn't trust anyone, ever. She was the most paranoid person I ever met.

It drove Jo crazy. "I can't get anything from her!" she told my mum once. "I don't mean money – Lord knows, I don't want money. But my birth certificate! Family photographs! The bank account that I know for a *fact* was set up for me when I was six months old. She hides *everything*. I don't think even *she* knows where half of it is. I think the old cow just enjoys knowing Dad and I will never get our hands on it."

"Hides how?" Mum said. "You mean in a bank or something?"

"Ha!" Jo said. "If only. No, safety-deposit boxes, secret locations, the whole works. We found one buried in the wall when we were building the extension. Actually cemented into the brickwork. Mum was furious. I think she'd forgotten she'd even put it there. She tried to pretend she didn't know anything about it, but honestly! She designed that house."

"Why doesn't she want you to have it?" Jonathan said. It didn't make any sense to me either. Auntie Irene had loads of money.

"Oh . . ." Jo shook her head. "She thinks Dad will divorce her and run off with the cash. Which, to be fair, he might. He's a slimy bastard, Dad."

The last time I saw Auntie Irene was at Mum's funeral.

Afterwards she beckoned me over. "I've got something for you," she said. "Don't tell your brothers or they'll all want something, and I'm not wasting my money on computer games or plastic tat."

She rummaged in her bag and handed me a small velvet box. Inside was a chain with a small silver locket on the end of it.

"When your mother was a little girl, she used to love playing with my jewellery," she said. "It used to drive me mad. Anyway . . . I always wanted her to have some of my jewellery when I died. So I thought perhaps you might like it instead. If you don't, let me know, and I'll take it back."

But I did like it. I never wore it, because it was about a hundred years old and kind of weird and more the sort of thing Dobby the House Elf would wear than something an actual kid would, but I liked that Auntie Irene had given it to me and not to Jonathan, and I liked that my mum had liked it.

I liked Auntie Irene too. Even if she was grumpy and a bit mad. Plenty of great people are a bit mad sometimes. Like Gandalf. Or Gonzo. Or Gandhi. I'd rather be fantastic and mad than boring and sane. Any day.

SAYING GOODBYE

We went to visit Auntie Irene on Saturday evening after Jonathan finished work. Gran gave us a ginormous spider plant and a chocolate cake to give to Auntie Irene. I took the plant. Jonathan took the cake tin, and Davy took a model of the Millennium Falcon made out of random bits of Lego.

"Can we eat the cake yet?" said Davy.

"*No*," I said. "It's a present. You have to give it to Auntie Irene and then look hopeful and then she'll say, 'Oh, what a lovely big cake, you must have a slice.'"

"We could just eat it and not give any to her," said Davy. But I told him stealing wasn't allowed.

We took the bus to the hospital. Auntie Irene had her own little room. It was sort of nice actually, much nicer than I'd expected. There were lots of get-well cards all along the windowsill, and on her table, so she could see them. It was all very hospital-y – hospital bed, with curtains round it, and a wipe-clean floor for unexpected vomit. But it was small and quiet and peaceful.

Auntie Irene was lying on her back in bed. She looked much smaller than the last time I'd seen her, shockingly smaller. Her white hair sat flatly against her cheeks, soft and fluffy, making her whole face look unexpectedly small and sad. She looked thinner than the last time I'd seen her too, and weirdly greyer. Like someone had come and sucked out the solid, colourful person she really was and left this snakeskin body in the bed.

Jo and Uncle Evan were both at the hospital when we got there. They looked a bit surprised to see us, like they were expecting a grown-up to have come with us or something.

"We're here because Gran can't come," I said, before they could say anything. Jonathan had gone shy. Jonathan is weirdly shy about loads of stuff. "She asked if we could come instead, so we did. And because we wanted to see Auntie Irene, obviously."

Auntie Irene didn't look like she wanted to see us. She looked asleep. Or possibly dead.

"Oh," said Jo. "Well. It's very nice to see you. Isn't it nice, Dad?" She gave me an encouraging smile.

Uncle Evan grunted. He didn't look like he thought it was nice. I started to wish we'd just eaten Gran's cake and not come.

"We brought you cake," said Jonathan. "And a plant."

The chocolate cake had slid to one side of the tin, and the icing had got squashed when Jonathan dropped it on the bus. Uncle Evan gave it this horrified look, like, *You expect me to eat* that?

Jo said, "Oh, that's so lovely of you, Jonathan, thank you."

"It's from Gran," said Jonathan. "I didn't make it."

And then there was an awkward pause.

Nobody seemed to know what to say next.

Davy leaned against me and whispered in my ear. "Can we eat the cake now?"

"Shh," I whispered back, though I was wondering that myself. "Don't be so rude."

"What does he want?" said Jo. She looked pleased to have something to talk about, I thought.

"He wants to know if he can have some cake," I said hopefully.

Uncle Evan made an angry noise. He got up and banged out of the room.

Jonathan and I looked at each other. "Was that me?" I said. "Did I upset him?"

"Oh . . ." Jo sighed. "No, of course you didn't, Holly. He's just . . . well, with Mum being ill . . ."

"We don't have to have cake," I said. "It's for your mum. We don't mind."

"No, cake is a good idea," said Jo. She got up. "I'll go and see if I can find a knife."

"I'll come too," said Jonathan hastily. I expect he was going to apologize for us or something, although *I* didn't see that we'd done anything that wrong.

Davy and I were left alone with Auntie Irene. We sat and watched her.

"Do you think she's going to die?" Davy whispered.

"Now?" I said. "No." I hoped not, anyway. They wouldn't have left her with us if she was going to die, would they? They wouldn't, right?

Davy padded over to the bed and peered at Auntie Irene. "Why does she look like that?" he said.

"Like what?" I said, though I knew really.

Davy gave a sort of one-armed shrug.

"She's sick," I said, helplessly.

And then Auntie Irene opened her eyes.

Davy made an "Agh!" noise, and jumped back.

I wanted to laugh, but I didn't. I was a bit scared too. "Hello," I said, nervously. I figured that was probably safe. Either she didn't know we were there, and it wouldn't make any difference, or she did, and she'd be pleased. "Hello, Auntie Irene. It's Holly and Davy."

Auntie Irene gazed at us. Her mouth moved but no sound came out. Davy retreated so far away from the bed that he bumped into my legs. He was staring at her like she was something evil coming up from the sewers to kill him.

I remembered what Jo had said, about the stroke, and how Auntie Irene couldn't talk. Like Grandad. *How awful*, I thought. Imagine waking up and whole bits of your body not working any more.

"Har–" she said. "Haar–"

"Are you trying to say Holly?" I said, hopefully. I decided that was a better option than some of the alternatives – *help me*, say, or *ha ha ha*.

To my surprise, she started jerking her head, like she was nodding. I hadn't really believed that she was still in there. She'd looked pretty out of it to me.

"That's right," I said. Knowing that she knew who I was made me feel safer. I took her hand. The skin was loose and dry and white. There were brown speckles on the back of her hand, like water marks.

She pulled her hand away angrily. "Eya–" she said.

"What?" I said. I'm the person in our family who's happiest talking to people, and even I wasn't feeling very sure about this. "I don't know what you're try to say." I looked at the door. I wished Jonathan and Jo would come back.

"Eya eenu–" she said, and then she tossed her head in a little gesture of frustration. She started jabbing her hand at the bedside cabinet.

I was beginning to panic. "Shall I get Jo?" I said. She shook her head, furious, and continued jabbing. "You want something from here?" I pulled out the drawer. It was full of her things, things that I guess Uncle Evan and Jo had brought or unpacked from her handbag or something. "What is it? This?" I held up her earphones. "This?" A box of pills. "This?" A packet of Polo mints. "This?" I pulled out what looked like a book, and she

31

started to get really excited. She stopped jabbing and waved her hands about and beamed at me.

I looked at the thing in my hand. It was a photograph album, just a little one, the size of a single photograph, and probably with room for about twenty photos in it. It had green cardboard covers, and plastic sheaths inside for the photographs to sit in.

It surprised me, that Auntie Irene would have something like that. She wasn't the sort of old lady who didn't know how a computer worked. She made her living from technology. I'd have expected all her photographs to be digital ones, on a complicated double-encrypted data cloud somewhere.

I opened the photograph album, but she started shaking her head again.

She pushed the album towards me. "Eeyore – eeyore."

Davy started to giggle nervously. I knew just how he felt.

"I don't . . . I'm sorry, I don't know what you want me to do with this. Is it a present?"

She started nodding again.

Were you allowed to take presents from people with brain injuries? I wondered if I ought to tell Jo, or try and give it back or something, but Auntie Irene was looking more and more agitated, so I said, "OK. All right. Thank you. That's . . . I'll look at it later."

And I put it in my bag.

WHAT WAS IN THE
PHOTOGRAPH ALBUM

On the bus back to the station, I opened the photograph album. I was expecting pictures of my mum, or maybe me and Jonathan as babies. But the photographs were utterly bizarre. There was:

- A picture of Auntie Irene's living-room wall. Not her current living room, which had been extended so it was about twice the size and had a conservatory, but the one she'd had before.
- A picture of what looked like a railway siding. There was half a signal box, and the tail end of a railway carriage, with FATZ 93 scrawled over it in purple spray paint.
- A beach somewhere hot. A ridiculously bright

turquoise sea, a big blue sky, palm trees and little square huts on stilts, with roofs made of straw, or palm leaves or something.

- Another beach, a pebbly, British-looking one. Not even a beach really, a sort of little cove. A grey sea, some long, yellowish grass, a sky full of clouds.

- An office. Not a private office in someone's house with a big oak desk and a leather desktop like Uncle Evan had, but a scruffy, messy office with a cheap old desk with metal legs and scratched veneer, and an ancient-looking computer, and an in-tray with loads of papers all piled in a heap. The room had the look of an old house that had once been grand, but now wasn't. A bit like ours. There was a big high ceiling, with fancy moulding on it and a hole where a chandelier had probably once hung. The walls were painted horrible rice-pudding grey.

There were no people in any of the photos. They weren't even exciting artistic landscapes. They looked like the sort of photos you take just to test whether your camera is working. I couldn't work out why Auntie Irene even had the album with her in hospital. She must have been carrying it around in her handbag or something, and it had been unpacked into the drawer.

"I told you she was crazy," said Jonathan, when I

showed him the pictures. "I'd chuck them out if I were you."

But I didn't. I kept them. I didn't know Auntie Irene very well, but she wasn't stupid. And in all the time I knew her, she never did anything without a purpose.

WHEN I GROW UP

Science runs in our family. Jonathan likes' science, like Auntie Irene did, and so do I. In fact, when I grow up, I'm going to be a climate scientist. Not the sort of climate scientist who takes notes of how much hotter it's getting, but the sort who builds things, like Auntie Irene did. I'm going to build machines to take carbon out of the atmosphere, and machines to make renewable energy really cheaply, and machines to make the planet colder. Because even if you take all the carbon out of the atmosphere, the planet is already hotter than it ought to be, so the ice caps will probably keep melting. I think what we should probably do is build lots of really big air-conditioning units, but that will obviously be quite expensive and use lots of carbon, so we'll have to wait until I've designed amazing renewable energy sources. But I'll do it.

I am the most environmentally-friendly person in my family. I'm the one who nags Jonathan to recycle stuff, and made him get electricity from a green energy supplier, and I'm the person who always takes rucksacks to the supermarket so we don't have to get plastic bags. Actually, we are quite a green family. We don't go on foreign holidays, or own a car, and we wear all our clothes until they're falling to pieces. It's mostly because we're poor, though, not because we're super-ethical. But still.

Bad things happening to the planet is my biggest worry. I think we are probably all going to be dead by the time I am old, or if not dead, at least all crammed onto the North Pole and the South Pole, which will probably have palm trees on them. It makes me so scared and angry that people don't pay any attention to real, obvious, provable science, and still insist on flying in aeroplanes, and buying lots of clothes that they don't wear, and driving cars. It's like none of the grown-ups cares at all about people like Jonathan and Davy and me, who will have to live in the world they made.

It was Auntie Irene who helped me not be so scared, actually. I told her how worried about it I was, and she said the best thing to do with a worry was to find something to do about it, which is when I started nagging Jonathan about recycling and stuff. I said, if climate change was such a big worry, why weren't all the scientists working overtime trying to fix it? And she said that was a good question, and when I grew up I ought to do something about it.

So I'm going to.

GREAT PIVOTAL MOMENTS IN
BECOMING A WOMAN
(OR, JONATHAN AND DAVY IN A BRA SHOP)

The next day was Sunday, and I made Jonathan take me bra shopping. Normally, when you get your first bra, either your mum tells you you need one, or you tell your mum you want one. What happened to me was I noticed all the other girls in my year had one and I didn't. Well, all the girls except for Amber Hale, who looks about nine.

So, that night, when Jonathan came home, I said, "I need a bra."

Jonathan looked flummoxed. (Flummoxed is a good word to use about Jonathan.) "Are you sure?" he said. "I mean, define 'need'. Couldn't you be a sixties feminist and not bother?"

You'd think my brother had never *been* to secondary school.

"No," I said. "I need one. People at school are going to think it's weird if I don't."

Now Jonathan looked anxious. "Are they expensive?" he said. And then, "Do *I* have to come with you?"

"How should I know?" I said. "And yes, you totally do. I can't go on my own."

So I went with Jonathan and Davy instead. Because that was totally normal.

We went to BHS, because they do toys as well as bras, and Davy was already whining about having to spend his Sunday lingerie shopping. We went to the toy department first. They had a table with Lego on it for kids to play with, so Davy ran straight there and started building a spaceship. Jonathan and I mucked about pressing all the buttons on the toys with buttons and giving stupid names to the teddy bears, until the staff started glaring at us. So then we dragged Davy out and went down to Clothes.

Even a cheap department store like BHS has a fancy clothes bit. I tried on four different bridesmaid's dresses, and three different fancy bridesmaid shoes. I tried to get Jonathan to try on one of the wedding dresses but he wouldn't. He and Davy were just boring and played secret agents with the hats.

Eventually, I got sick of waiting. "Come on," I said. "I'm supposed to be buying a bra."

"So go and buy one then," said Jonathan. He adjusted his top hat in the mirror. "We'll be right here."

What, I was supposed to go to the lingerie department

40

on my own, grab a knicker-selling lady and tell her I wanted my first bra? No way.

"They'll think I'm *weird*!" I wailed. "They'll call social services! In twenty years' time I'll be depressed and alcoholic and telling a psychiatrist that my brother made me buy my first bra on my own! I'll write one of those books you see in supermarkets with sad black-and-white kids on the front of them and when I get to be interviewed on TV about it, I'll tell them this story, and then you'll get *hate mail* and I won't even care!"

Jonathan tipped his hat to one side so it sat at a jaunty angle. He probably thought this made him look cool and sophisticated. Unfortunately, he was wearing jeans with a big hole in the knee and a T-shirt with mathematical equations on it, so he just looked ridiculous.

"Jon-a-than," I wailed. This is supposed to be a significant day in a young girl's life! It's – like – a whatchamacallit – a rite of passage. Like a bat mitzvah, or confirmation, or being dumped in the Australian Outback on your own without any food and having to find your way home. Come *on*. It's an important mother-daughter bonding ritual."

"But we're not your mother," said Davy. He was wearing big woolly mittens with elephants on and an enormous pink hat with lace and flowers and feathers stuck on it.

"Well, you're the best I've got," I said.

We went to the lingerie section. It was totally weird. Lacy knickers, and weird stretchy elastic to wear under your clothes to make you look slimmer, and awful ugly bras with lace and frills on them.

Was that really what grown-ups wore?

Davy went straight to the tights rack. "Holly, look! Pink tights! And frog tights, look! Can I have frog tights?"

There were two Ladies Who Lingerie waiting at the door to the changing room. We went up to them.

"How many items?" said the lady, smiling at Davy, who was still wearing his enormous pink hat. "Are you going to a wedding, sweetheart?"

Davy shrank back against Jonathan's legs and shook his head.

Jonathan shot me a look of utter panic. "Er—"

"I need a bra," I said.

"OK," said the Lingerie Lady. "Do you need a fitting?"

"Er – yeah. I guess so."

That bit was weird, but not as weird as I'd worried it might be. The lady measured me, then went and found me bras in different sizes to try on. She stayed outside while I put them on, but came back in when I was done to see how well they fitted.

"You're still growing," she said. "So once they start getting a bit tight, you'll need to come and have another fitting."

"Right," I said. I was starting to panic a bit. I'd had a look at the price tag, and bras were expensive. How many was I supposed to buy? How often was I supposed to change them? Every day, like knickers? I had a whole drawerful of knickers, but you could buy them in multipacks from Asda. I tried to imagine Jonathan's face when I told him I needed a whole drawer of bras, but was probably going to grow out of them in a couple of months. How fast do breasts grow? And would the lady think I was a minger if I only bought a couple? Would she think it weird that I didn't already know this? Did she *already* think it weird that I was here with a big brother in a top hat and a little brother in a pink one?

"Um," I said. "Um. How many are you supposed to buy? Only . . ." I hesitated.

The Lingerie Lady smiled. "I'd just get two or three for now," she said. "They come in multipacks – go have a look."

I could have hugged her.

We went back outside. Davy was still wearing his flowery hat. He was trying on silk scarves from a silk-scarf rack, winding them round and round and round his neck until he looked like an Egyptian mummy whose mummifier had got bored halfway through making him. I glanced at the Lingerie Lady to see if she was angry, but she was still smiling. I wondered if she was going to ask where my mum was, but she didn't.

"Nice to have a brother who'll come shopping with you," she said, instead.

I smiled back. "Yeah," I said. "It is."

MUM

My mum's name was Theresa Kennet, or Tess for short. She was a policewoman, which sounds like it's all catching serial killers like on TV, but is actually mostly cordoning off bits of road when there's been a car crash and standing around being bored at London Pride, and protest marches, and arresting drunk people late at night when they're causing trouble.

My mum was little and fierce and funny. If she wanted something, she wouldn't shut up until she got it. I'm like that too. I'm the one of us who's most like her. But she was kind as well. She was great when you were sad, or scared, or lonely. She wasn't afraid of anything, not even really big drunk men. She told them what was what.

When my mum was young, she was a bit of a rebel.

She hitch-hiked all the way to Rome once, when she was nineteen. She lived in a squat for two years when she was sixteen, with her boyfriend, because she didn't have enough money to pay proper rent, and she kept having fights with my grandparents.

When she was twenty, she met Jonathan's dad and got pregnant. And then she decided she had to get a proper job, and that's when she joined the police. Some of her friends from the squat thought she was awful for doing that, because they thought the police were thugs who just did what they were told and beat up innocent people who weren't doing anything wrong. But my mum knew the police weren't going to go away, and she knew they were useful for things like car crashes and murders. And she thought it would be a good idea if nice people signed up to be police, as well as thugs, and then maybe there'd be less thuggery and more niceness.

My mum was a very good policeperson. She worked hard at her exams, even though she was looking after baby Jonathan on her own. She was a sergeant when she died.

When Jonathan was four, she met Davy's and my dad. His name was Steve, and he was a nurse. Male nurses on telly are young and sexy and usually gay. (Apart from Charlie on *Casualty*.) My dad wasn't young – he was thirty-two. And he had red hair and a beard. But he was nice, and kind, and he picked broken glass out of my mum's arm when a drunk person threw a broken bottle at her, and didn't laugh when she swore at him because it hurt so much. And then she said, "I owe you a drink for that," and he sort of shrugged and said, "Just doing my job," which my mum liked. My mum liked people who liked their jobs and worked hard at them and were good at them. She always told Jonathan and me, "It doesn't matter if you don't earn lots of money, but you should be proud of what you do, and do it well." And my mum and dad both were, and did.

My mum said she fancied my dad the first time she met him. I asked if he fancied her too, and she laughed and said, "Him? No! He was too scared." My mum could be a bit scary at times. I could imagine her swearing at my poor dad in A&E.

Anyway, so the next time my mum went into A&E – escorting a prisoner! – she saw my dad again, and this time she made sure she got his phone number. And then they got married, and had me, and Davy, and moved into the flat we still live in now, and they were very happy, and everything was lovely.

I was six when my dad died. He had a burst appendix. I still remember him, but only in bits. Like, I have memories with him in them, but I can't really remember what it felt like to have a dad, if that makes sense. Or, I can, but only like I can remember what it felt like to be little.

After my dad died, we lived with my mum, and mostly everything was still lovely. It was a bit weird, because when you're in the police you have to work lots of nights, and we couldn't go to a childminder's in the middle of the night. So when I was very little, we used to go to Gran and Grandad's house quite a lot. And then after Grandad had his stroke and they moved to an old people's home, Jonathan had to look after us.

I was eleven when my mum died. She had stomach cancer. My Auntie Grace came over from New Zealand, which was weird, especially because our flat is tiny, so she had to sleep in the living room. And she kept telling Jonathan he ought to be doing more to help out in the house, which was super-weird, because Jonathan never did housework. I mean, he did lots of babysitting – and he helped with the washing-up if Mum asked him to, but only with lots of grumbling, and usually several hours after she'd asked. So when Auntie Grace started telling him he was supposed to be doing all the housework, *and* Mum was sick, *and* we had this strange lady we hardly knew living in our house, it was a bit much.

Usually eleven year olds don't get much say in where they live, except maybe if their parents divorce or something, but because we didn't have a dad, we were always pretty involved in decisions Mum made. Things like where we went on holiday, and what colour we should paint the kitchen, and whether I went to the secondary school down the road or the fancy new academy with the computer suites and the music centre, and the weird classrooms with glass walls and no doors.

So when Mum knew she was going to die, she sat me down and talked to me about where I wanted to live.

She said I could go to New Zealand and live with Auntie Grace. And I'd probably have to share a bedroom with my cousin Sadie, who I'd never met, and there might not be much money, because two sudden extra kids are quite expensive, and it was a long way away on the other side of the world, of course. And we wouldn't see much of Jonathan, because he already had a place at university and it was too late to apply in New Zealand, so he'd stay here, and maybe come over in the summer holidays. But Auntie Grace had said she was happy to have us, if that's what we wanted, and New Zealand was very beautiful, and it would all be a big adventure.

Or, she said, I could stay here and Jonathan would look after me. I was a bit surprised when she said that, because I thought Jonathan was a kid, not a grown-up. I mean, he was always bigger than me, but he was still a *kid*, you know? But she said because he was eighteen it would be OK, and she could rewrite her will to make him our legal guardian, and she'd already talked to Jonathan and he'd said he was willing to do it. And it wouldn't be easy, but we could still go to the same schools, and live in the same flat, and still see Gran and Grandad, and I could keep doing all the things I already did, like being a library monitor, and being on the netball team. And she thought it would be all right, but only if I wanted to.

I suppose I ought to have thought about it a bit before I answered. But I didn't. I definitely want to go to New Zealand one day, and visit Hobbiton, and climb some of those cool-looking mountains that they climb in the

Lord of the Rings films. (Except I am against aeroplanes because of my carbon footprint, but I could take the Trans-Siberian Railway across Russia and then a boat, which would be far cooler anyway.) But I didn't want to live there. And I didn't want to live with Auntie Grace, who told me off for leaving my clothes on my bedroom floor, and told Jonathan he ought to be doing all the washing-up. My whole life is here, in this little corner of London. I don't know anything else.

So I told Mum I wanted to stay. And Davy said the same thing. And that was that.

AUNTIE IRENE AGAIN

Jo rang after school on Thursday. Davy and I were building a Lego train set all the way through the kitchen. We didn't have enough train track to make the railway (Davy's Lego train only came with a rubbish little circle of track) but the kitchen had washable tiles, so we just drew track straight onto the floor with felt tip.

"Holly," said Jo, when I answered the phone. "Is Jonathan there?"

"No, he's at work," I said. "Are you OK? Is Auntie Irene OK?"

"Not really," said Jo. "I'm sorry, Holly. She died last night."

"Oh," I said. "I'm sorry." I didn't know quite how to feel. I knew I ought to be sad, because I liked Auntie Irene, but I didn't really feel sad, because actually I didn't know her very well. I felt removed-sad, like the way you feel when something sad happens on the news, or to one of your friends. I also felt a bit weird that I was allowed to have this conversation with Jo. Dead relations are *definitely* not something you're supposed to have to deal with, when you're twelve.

"The funeral will be next week sometime," said Jo. "But I know Jonathan works, so I'll understand if you guys can't come. Tell him Mum wouldn't want him to lose money for her sake. Unless he wants to come, of course."

"I'll tell him," I said. Jonathan doesn't get sick pay or holiday pay, so whenever he has to take time off work, like if one of us is ill, or it's Davy's nativity play or something, he doesn't earn enough to pay the rent. I wouldn't have thought someone like Jo, with a proper job and all the rest of it, would have understood that, but she did.

"OK," said Jo. "And, Holly, I need to talk to him about Mum's will. Tell him to ring me, will you?"

"Auntie Irene's will!" I sat straight upright, I was so excited. "Has she left us some money?" Auntie Irene was loaded, everyone knew that. Maybe she'd left us a million pounds. Maybe she'd left us a house!

"Not exactly," said Jo. "Honestly, Holly, I shouldn't have said anything. Please don't get excited. Just tell Jonathan to call me when he gets in, will you?"

But of course I did get excited. I'd never been left anything in a will before. Mum left all her money to Jonathan, to spend on boring things like rent.

I wondered what she'd left us.

A car? A villa in Spain? A yacht? (I wasn't sure why Auntie Irene would leave us a yacht, but I couldn't see Uncle Evan using one. Perhaps she figured we'd be able to use it more, being young. We could totally use a yacht. We could go and live on it, and Jonathan could give up being a waiter and get a job taking people out sailing for the afternoon. How hard could it be? You just had to put the wind behind the sail, right?)

Davy was just as excited as I was.

"Maybe she's left me a bike!" he said.

"A bike?" I said. "Why would Auntie Irene own a kids' bike?"

"She might!" said Davy. "Or – or – or – maybe she's left me some treasure, and we could spend it on a bike!"

"I didn't know you wanted a bike," I said.

Davy hugged himself as tight as he could. "I want one more than *anything*," he said, all round-eyed and serious. It was the first I'd heard of it.

Jonathan wasn't nearly as excited as we were, but he did call Jo back. Davy and I tried to eavesdrop, but he didn't say anything exciting. It was all, "Yes . . . yes . . . yes, I understand . . . yes, of course."

"She's coming round," he said when he'd put the phone down.

"Here?" I said, alarmed. The flat was a mess. Every piece of crockery we owned was dirty, and most of it was in the living room. And we hadn't taken the rubbish out in ages, so the kitchen smelt. And any bit of floor that didn't have rubbish or dirty plates on it had Davy's Lego railway winding its way carefully and economically through all the obstructions, Lego houses and signal boxes wedged in amongst the piles of paper and chip boxes, like the Lego people were trying to build a city in a future world completely overrun with mess, like the one in *WALL-E*.

"God no," said Jonathan. "We're going for coffee."

Jo rang the buzzer and waited for us to come down. She was unusually flustered. And she looked a bit alarmed when she saw Davy and me come out with Jonathan.

"Oh," she said. "Er – hello, Holly. Jonathan, are you sure . . .?"

"We want cake!" Davy said, before Jonathan could say anything. "And ice cream!"

"Oh," said Jo. "Right. Well – of course."

She took us to the Moroccan restaurant on the corner with the hookah pipes which Mum would never let us try. She let us order cake, and ice cream, and milkshakes, and she sat there while we ate, looking worried and miserable. That was my first clue that maybe we hadn't been left a house.

"The thing is," she said. "Well Mum really liked you three. I know she did. She liked your mum too. Your mum used to come and stay for holidays when we were little, and Mum always liked her. I know she felt bad about the way things were for you . . . but, well, she never gave money to people, ever. She thought people should solve their own problems, not expect hand-outs from relations. Even when I was little, I had to earn all my own pocket money and win scholarships to school and things like that."

Jonathan was looking down at his coffee cup. He was looking like he wanted to run away and hide, but he couldn't, because Davy was kneeling on his chair, sucking chocolate milkshake through his straw like this was the most exciting thing that had ever happened to him, ever.

I was getting a bit bored with all this miserableness when we didn't even have anything to be miserable about yet. (Well. Jo did. Her mum had just died.) "So she hasn't left us anything?" I said.

"Holly!" said Jonathan.

"Sort of," said Jo. She rubbed her eyes. "I'm sorry," she said. "It's been a horrible week. You know what Mum was like. Totally paranoid. The last few years, she got even worse. She was convinced Dad was going to steal all her money. And she was convinced we were trying to take it and spend it on the boys. Just because I asked her once if she'd help out with Noah's school fees. Which was a huge mistake. Of course."

"Did you like her?" I asked. I couldn't imagine having a mum like that. In my experience mums were just . . . mums. Nice. Kind. Sensible.

"Oh, I don't know," said Jo. "It's complicated, and sad, and I'm sorry, Holly, but I don't really want to talk about it right now."

I opened my mouth to point out that she'd started it. Then Jonathan kicked me, and I shut it again.

"Anyway," Jo said. "The important thing is, when

55

your mum was a little girl, Mum apparently told her she could have all the jewellery after Mum was gone. We used to play with it when we were little. *So*, when Tess died last year, Mum changed the will, leaving the jewellery to you."

"Oh," said Jonathan. He looked a bit taken aback. "That's – that's – um – very nice of her."

"Is it worth money?" I said. Jonathan glared at me. "I'm sorry," I said. "I don't want to be rude. But – like, your mum had old-lady jewellery. And Davy and Jonathan are boys. So – I mean – it's lovely that Auntie Irene thought of us – but . . ."

"It's all right," said Jo. "I'm sure she expected you to sell it. And yes, the jewellery is worth a lot of money. There are a couple of really beautiful pieces. This isn't the jewellery she wore every day – she left that to me, because she knew I'm the sentimental one. This is the stuff she wore to gala dinners and press launches. Some of it is ridiculous."

"But there's a problem," said Jonathan.

"Yes," said Jo. "We can't find any of her paperwork. She's got all sorts of shares, and investments, but we don't know with whom, or what her customer ID numbers are, or anything. We can't even find the deeds to the house. And the jewellery was always kept in a safe in her dressing room, but it vanished when she retired. That was two years ago. We thought she'd put it all in the bank, but apparently not. I'm sorry, Jonathan."

"But," I said, "she can't have sold it, can she? I mean,

if it vanished two years ago, and she changed her will last year, that means she still owns it, right?"

"I suppose so," said Jo. She sounded tired. Jonathan was giving me the evils. "Look, I don't know what to say, Holly. I'm sorry. It really could be anywhere. She had all sorts of paperwork hidden in a safe in the living-room wall. And I'm almost certain she hid something in that house she used to own in Polynesia. I mean, Polynesia, for heaven's sake! Lord knows where she put the jewellery. I wish I had better news for you, but honestly, I think you should just be pleased that she remembered you, and leave it at that."

"But!" I said. "But—"

"Holly," said Jonathan. "That's enough. Eat your cake and be quiet. I mean it."

"But—" I said, and he half sat up like he was about to grab my ear and drag me out of the restaurant. I shut up and chomped down on my cake and tried to pretend like I was miserable.

But inside I wasn't miserable.

Inside I was turning somersaults on my own personal trampoline.

You see, I knew just where Auntie Irene had hidden our jewellery. I was sure I did.

I KNOW WHERE AUNTIE IRENE
HID THE TREASURE. I DO!

I waited until we were outside the Moroccan restaurant and had waved goodbye to Jo. Then I grabbed Jonathan's arm. "I know where the jewellery is!" I said.

Jonathan gave me his *why did God give me a sister?* look.

"No, I do!" I said. Jonathan leant against the bus shelter while I rummaged in my bag. "Look!" I said. I flapped the album in his face.

"OK," said Jonathan. "Calm down. Jesus. How old are you – eight?"

"Yeah, yeah," I said. "Look at this!" I riffled through the album until I found the picture I wanted: Auntie Irene's living room, with the drinks cabinet and a vase of flowers and photographs and framed newspaper cuttings on the wall. "That's where Jo said they found the safe!

Remember? So these must be pictures of where Auntie Irene hid the rest of her safes! So she wouldn't forget where she put them! *That's* why she gave it to me!"

"Hold on," said Jonathan. He took the book and turned the pages slowly. I bounced up and down impatiently.

Davy peered over the edge of the cover like a hopeful gnome. "That's where Auntie Irene hid her treasure?" he said.

"Yep," I said. I gave another little bounce. "It's like the Moors Murderers! I saw this TV programme about them – they killed loads of people and then buried their bodies on the moors, and they took photos of the graves and went and had picnics on them. This is just the same!" I saw Jonathan's expression. "Only, you know, gold and stuff, not bodies. Probably. Although maybe bodies actually, knowing Uncle Evan."

Jonathan didn't say anything. He looked through the photograph album very slowly and carefully, studying each photograph in turn.

"Maybe," he said, in the end. "But, Holly, these are just pictures of beaches and railway lines. How are you going to find out where they are? There are still bodies of people the Moors Murderers killed that the police haven't found. And their photos were all of one moor! These could be anywhere!"

"We'll find them," I said, confidently. "We'll take them to the Maker Space on Sunday! There are loads of geniuses there. If anyone can find out where these photos were taken, they can."

WHAT THE MAKER SPACE WAS

So, imagine you're best friends with an inventor. Not just one inventor – about a hundred real, mad-scientist, evil-genius type inventors. The kid on TV programmes who knows how to hack computers and build bombs out of glue and kitchen foil. Inspector Gadget, or that guy who invented time travel in *Back to the Future*.

Now imagine *all* the mad scientists in TV programmes got together and pooled their money to buy the biggest and best mad-scientist laboratory they could. This thing is nearly *warehouse*-sized. It's on two floors. It's got classrooms, where you can run lock-picking classes and lessons in how to use metal-cutters. It's got all the biggest and most awesome equipment from the best sort of CDT lab, plus wood and metal and wires, and 3D printers, and desks, and lots and lots of interesting people making interesting (and mostly legal) things. There are biology fanatics, who are doing DNA tests on random bits of food to find out if they're really what they say they are. There are people building robots, and people building rockets, and people just trying to help other people make the things they want to make. There's even a lightsabre, for when people get bored of making things and want to mess around.

That's the London Maker Space.

Jonathan joined first, about two years ago. He got interested in computer programming and building stuff – he programmed one of those boxes that lets you play music and films out of your telly. Then he made Davy a robot that would read his favourite stories when he pushed the button with the right picture on it, because Mum was getting fed up of reading *Charlie and the Chocolate Factory* over and over. And then Gran and Grandad bought him a year's membership as a Christmas present, which was more than they usually spent on us, but Grandad really liked building things too, so I think he thought it was worth it.

When Mum died, Jonathan stopped going for a bit, because he had us to look after, and things got complicated. But then Alex and Jen, who are mates of his, told him he should still come, and it didn't matter about Davy and me, because we could come too.

"Little people!" Jen said. "Baby geeks! Bring them along! We'll teach them to take over the world!"

Which is sort of what happened.

There are lots and lots of people who belong to the Maker Space. Some of them are grumpy and unfriendly, and some of them are weird, and some of them are busy and important, so I don't know everyone. But *most* of them are totally friendly and totally clever and totally lovely.

They all know us, of course, because there aren't many teenagers who turn up with a six- and eleven-year-old brother and sister, who they look after full time, and want to know if they're allowed to let them play with saws. We were kind of noticeable.

The thing about the Maker Space is that the whole point is helping. People come in all the time and go, "I'm trying to make a rocket, but I've gone wrong," and everyone just wanders over and pokes at it and makes suggestions until they've got it working. So when people cottoned on to the fact that what Jonathan really needed was someone to look after us so he could go and build things in peace, they were totally cool with that.

Davy and I have loads of friends at the Maker Space now. Grown-up friends, obviously. There's Alex and Jen, who are married and come from Canada. There's Peter, who's about fifty, and has a big red bushy beard, and is building a spaceship. A very small one. It's a tiny cube, and he's going to send it up into space and programme it to take pictures and go and say hello to the International Space Station. And . . . oh, lots of people.

There really are lock-picking classes too. Every month on a Wednesday.

FIND A PICTURE, PICK IT UP

The other reason I knew the Maker Space would be able to help me with Auntie Irene's photographs is because they're all about solving stuff. Nobody ever says, "That's impossible." They all go, "Ooh, interesting problem," and then spend half an hour debating all the different possible ways of solving it. It gets a bit boring when they're talking on and on and on and on about code, but then they go off and type, and mix stuff together, and a couple of months later, the problem is solved.

As soon as we got there on Sunday, I ran over to Jen. Jen is awesome. Her job is designing computer games *for real*. She has bright pink hair and purple Doc Martens, and she's really smart and kind as well.

"Jen!" I said when I saw her. I told her all about Auntie Irene, and the photographs and the money. "There has to be a way to find out where photos are taken, hasn't there? There has to be!"

Jen was a much better listener than Jonathan. "Hmm," she said. "I'm not sure, Holly. I think Jonathan has a point. I mean . . . I guess you could put them on the internet and see if anyone can recognize them. I dunno – hope it goes viral. It might. I mean, that's a cool story, you guys looking after one another. But I wouldn't hold out much hope."

"How do you mean?" I asked. "You mean like those people on Facebook who share pictures of lost cats?"

"That's right," said Jen. "It's called 'crowdsourcing'. You make a website with your information on it, then you get everyone you know to share it, and you see if anyone who sees it knows where the pictures are. It's worth a try, anyway."

"OK," I said. "Cool."

And then I went off to help Peter finish his spaceship. You can make websites anytime.

IN WHICH I START TRYING TO FIND THE TREASURE

I told my friend Sizwe about the website idea at school on Monday. I have lots of friends – that sounds show-offy, but it isn't. In fact it's sort of the opposite of show-offy, because what I mean is, there's a whole gang of us at school who hang around together at break time, and I'm one of them. But that doesn't mean I'm exactly *friends* with all of them. I mean, I sit with Sufiya and Kali in history, and I went to Kali's birthday party, but that doesn't mean I'd call either of them up if I had a big life problem or anything.

The person I'd probably call up if I had a big life problem – I don't normally call up *any* of my friends if I have a big life problem, I don't normally tell *anybody* – but if I did, the person I'd call up would be Sizwe. Sizwe's great. He's little and happy, he's like a rubber ball – he's always bouncing. He never laughs at me, like Sufiya and

Kali do sometimes. I don't have a best friend, but if I did it would be Sizwe. Sizwe, then Neema, then Issy.

Sizwe's the only friend I told about Auntie Irene's treasure, and how I wanted to make a website to help us find it. But Neema was listening and when she heard about it, she got all excited and wanted to help too.

I know how to make websites. That was one of the first bits of programming I learnt. I didn't bother making one for the pictures, though. I just set up a blog on one of those sites that lets you set up blogs. This is what my blog said:

PLEASE CAN YOU HELP US?

We are a sister and two brothers, Jonathan, Holly and Davy. Jonathan is nineteen, Holly is twelve and Davy is seven. We have been looking after ourselves since our mum died last year.

Last week we got left some jewellery in our Auntie Irene's will. But Auntie Irene was kind of weird and she hid the jewellery, along with lots of other stuff which belongs to Uncle Evan and her daughter, Jo.

BUT, WE THINK WE KNOW WHERE THE TREASURE IS! Auntie Irene gave me these photographs, and I think that's where she hid the boxes. Which is where you all come in! Do you know any of the places in these pictures?

PLEASE TELL ALL YOUR FRIENDS TO
LOOK AT THIS WEBSITE AND HELP, AND
PLEASE TELL US IN THE COMMENTS
IF YOU KNOW WHERE ANY OF THESE
PLACES ARE! THANK YOU! I LOVE YOU!

Holly Kennet

And then I scanned in the photos on the school scanner and put the pictures on the blog.

"That is so awesome," said Neema. "Now what do we do?"

"Now we have to tell everyone about it," I said. "You have to send it to everyone you know."

"And then it goes viral!" said Sizwe. "And you become internet superheroes, and celebrities get involved, and everyone shares it, and you find out where the treasure is hidden, and become millionaires, and move to a Caribbean island somewhere and live happily ever after."

This is why I like Sizwe. He's the anti-Jonathan.

We put the website up on our Facebook pages and emailed it to everyone in our address books, and I sent it to everyone on the London Maker Space email list, and Sizwe sent it to the football team, and Neema put it up on the London Parkour Network site, and then Sizwe got his mum to send it to all the people whose offices her cleaning company cleaned, and Neema got her dad to send it to everyone on the London Edible Gardens email list, which was huge.

And then we waited.

People went and looked at the website all day and all evening. Some of them left comments. Every time there was a new comment, I got hopeful that it would be someone who recognized the pictures, but it never was. It was always people saying things like "No idea, sorry." Or "Great website – good luck, Holly." Which was nice, but not very helpful. A couple of people must have sent it to their friends, or at least shared it on Facebook, and at first I was really hopeful that it was going to go viral and half the internet would see it, but it didn't. The day after that, we only got a couple of new comments. And there were none the next day, or the day after that.

I sent Jen an email and asked her to tell everyone to share the website with their friends, but she wouldn't.

"People will only share it if they want to. You've already asked them once, Holl."

Which was a typical grown-up non-answer. This mattered! It *really* mattered. It mattered too much to be polite about.

We went to the Maker Space again on Sunday. Several people wanted to talk to me about my website. Even people who normally never spoke to me. We were sitting having lunch when some guy I sort of half knew came up to us and said, "Are you the kid who's looking for treasure?" Which was a bit of a stupid question, since we were the *only* kids who ever came there.

"Yeah," I said. "Did you share my website with your friends? Did you? If you didn't, do it now."

"Holly," said Jonathan. In an *I'm so fed up of looking after my brother and sister* voice.

"We were supposed to share it?" said the guy. His name was Keith, I was fairly sure. He was older than most of Jonathan's friends – proper grown-up old, older than Mum. He had thick grey hair, and a beer belly. He was eating a sausage roll in a paper bag and dropping flaky pastry all over the table.

"*Yes*," I said, ignoring Jonathan. "Look, I'll show you." And I showed him the website on his phone. I made him read it all the way through, and I explained about Auntie Irene again. "You're supposed to tell everyone in your address book about it, and then it'll become a virus."

"I can do better than that," said Keith. He scrolled the page up until it showed the most boring picture of the lot, the one of the railway siding. "I know some people who'll be able to tell you where that's taken," he said.

"How?" I asked.

"Well," Keith said. "There are all sorts of identifying marks. The signal box. The rails. The carriages – they give you a date for the photograph, and that's Network South East stock, so that narrows the field some more."

Keith was into trains. I knew that. He was always building trees and houses and miniature nuclear reactors for his model train sets.

"There are a couple of online forums I could post that picture on if you want me to," he said.

"Yes!" I said. "Yes, yes, yes, yes, yes!"

At last!

71

THE AWESOME POWER
OF THE INTERNET

All that next day at school, I couldn't stop thinking about Keith and his train-loving friends. Had they found out where our treasure was? Keith had sounded so confident. Surely he must have found something? He must have, mustn't he?

I didn't have the sort of mobile you could check the internet on. I was pretty much the only kid in my year group who didn't. I had Mum's old mobile phone, which was about a hundred years old and couldn't even take photographs. So I had to wait until me and Davy got home to check my email.

I'm allowed to use Jonathan's laptop while he's at work. I turned it on, while Davy ran over to play with his Lego. There was an email from Keith.

Dear Holly,

I posted your picture on a couple of railway sites I belong to. Everyone was very interested in your photograph. From the size of the tracks, the type of signal box, the livery of the train in shot, and what we could see of the rest of the sidings, we believe we've identified the track shown in the photograph as part of a disused goods yard on a track about forty minutes out of Victoria.

A friend of mine, Neil Carter, lives not far from where your photograph was taken, and would be happy to show you the exact location of the signal box. His email address is below.

I hope you find what you're looking for.

Keith

I shrieked.

"Davy! We've found where one of Auntie Irene's photos was taken!" I grabbed Davy's hands and danced him round. Davy, who had no idea what I was talking about, danced along anyway.

"We found it, we found it!" he said. Of course, we hadn't actually found the *treasure*, but I'm not sure he realized that. Davy likes it when the people he loves are happy.

I went straight online, before Jonathan could stop me, and put a new post on my blog.

> WE FOUND WHERE ONE OF THE BOXES IS!
> THANK YOU, KEITH APPLEBY. WE HAVEN'T
> BEEN TO DIG UP THE TREASURE YET BUT
> WE WILL.

I got loads of comments. Loads of people going "Wow!" and "Good luck!" and "OMG Holly THAT IS SO COOL, YOU HAVE TO TELL US WHAT HAPPENS!" Everyone at school thought it was awesome. Well, Issy and Neema and Sizwe did, anyway. Sizwe especially.

"Oh my God," he kept saying. "How loaded was your Auntie Irene? Could she have diamonds and emeralds and stuff in there? Will you go and live in a beach house in Los Angeles with your own swimming pool? Will you ever talk to us again?"

I showed Jonathan the comments on my website when he came home, but he just grunted. He is such a pessimist. Honestly! I have to do all the work around here. If it was up to Jonathan, we'd just quietly starve to death.

In shoes that didn't fit.

He couldn't ignore all the people who wanted to talk to him at the Maker Space, though. Actually, most of the grown-ups weren't that interested either. But Jen was, of course, and Alex, and Keith was proud as Punch. (Or is Punch pleased? I can't remember.) He was full of practical advice for the best way to get onto railway land without being arrested or getting stuck in a hedge, and how important it was not to walk on the tracks and get electrocuted. (Like we would.) He brought some fluorescent jackets we could wear, so we would look like line workers and not attract attention.

"Keith," I said, impressed, "you are a secret master criminal." Keith chuckled and looked a bit embarrassed. "Got me the best collection of amateur railway photography in greater London, those did," he said. And then he went over all shy and went off to talk rockets with Alex.

Jen came over and gave me a hug. "Well done!" she said. "When are you going to go and dig the treasure up?"

"We're not," I told her. "Jonathan thinks it's all a load of rubbish. He won't even let us go and *see*!"

"Oh, Jonathan," said Jen. "Aren't you even a little bit curious?"

Jonathan threw up his hands. "Look!" he said. "Just look!" He took the photograph album from the table, where I'd left it after showing Keith the other photographs. "Look at this. Look how much grass there is in that picture. Let's say we don't get arrested for trespassing, or run over by a train. How are we even going to know where to dig? We don't even own spades!"

At that, everyone suddenly got very helpful. Keith and Jen both offered to lend us spades, and Alex went to look up how to make a metal detector online.

"No! Wait! We're fine!" Jonathan said, but it was too

late. Me and Alex and Davy spent the whole morning making a metal detector out of a radio and a broom handle sawn off a broom from the cleaning cupboard and a piece of wood and some wire. It worked too. We practised with it all the way home, and we detected three sets of railings, five bins, two Coke cans, a penny, and the number 47 bus.

"We *have* to go now!" I said, and Jonathan groaned.

"All right!" he said. "Fine! But if we get arrested, you're taking the fall. OK? Davy and me are counting on you to distract the cops while we make a run for it."

THE JOURNEY BEGINS

We went to find the treasure the next weekend. Jonathan, Davy and I.

As the train moved out of the station, I started to get excited. I hardly ever go anywhere any more. Not on an adventure like this. When Mum was alive, we used to do adventures – to Kew Gardens, or the National History Museum, or to the pantomime. Jonathan's idea of a good time is watching telly or messing about on the internet. Mostly, when Mum was alive, I used to moan about being dragged round Kew Gardens. But now we never go anywhere, I kind of miss it.

"Say goodbye to Victoria," a mother on the train was saying to her little girl.

"Goodbye, Victoria!" the girl said, like she was talking to a friend, not a railway station. "Goodbye, London!"

"I missed the train," a woman was saying into her mobile phone. "Just by a minute. Still, they're every hour, aren't they?" I wondered if she was lying, and if so, why?

There wasn't much to see out of the window. The railway track was closed in with tall brick walls. The bricks were small and old and stained black. Thick, heavy plants hung down over the tops, like jungle vines.

BEWARE OF TRAINS read a sign on the wall, like the trains were wild animals. *Too late!* I thought. *We've been swallowed by a train, and who knows what will happen next?*

The train chugged out of Victoria and over the river. Davy was fascinated. He pressed his nose up against the window. "Look!" he said. "Look, Holly!"

"Look at what?" I said.

"At. . ." Davy thought. Then he beamed. "At everything!"

There was lots to see. Building sites, office buildings, factories, tips, blocks of flats and Battersea Power Station. Joggers running down a street, all in a pack. A railway siding clogged with old, dead buddleia. Expensive-looking villas with conservatories and big leafy gardens, and terraced houses all in neat little rows. A SANITARY STEAM LAUNDRY like Mrs Ruggles had in *The Family from One End Street*, and old abandoned gasworks looming over the city like spider-monsters from Mars.

We passed a big park, and a posh-looking school with playing fields. The railway cutting grew bigger, with more trees and longer grass. The houses became more suburban. We passed a church spire, shaggy-looking allotments and a red digger.

"I can see why Keith likes railways," I said.

And then we were in the country. There were fields, and little woodland copses, birch trees and rowans with flashes of red rowanberries amongst the shiny green leaves. I was amazed. When did London stop? I must have missed it. I thought the end of London would be a sudden thing. One moment you'd be surrounded by shops and houses and advertising hoardings and tube trains, and the next it would be cows and fields and buttercups. But no. Here we were, and I'd never noticed it happening.

I'd better pay more attention on the way back in, I thought. *I must see just where it starts.* And then, *How weird to live somewhere that isn't London.* It felt like travelling to another country, or somewhere completely alien, like Narnia. It felt like travelling to Narnia.

TREASURE SIDING

The station was small. There was no ticket office, no café. There was a footbridge, and a bus shelter on each platform, and a machine with a big button you could press for information. That was it.

There was also a man waiting for us at the station platform. He was tall and skinny and sun-tanned, with thick white hair, waterproof gaiters and an expensive-looking camera around his neck. He was wearing another of Keith's fluorescent jackets, just like the ones Keith had given us.

"Neil," he said, holding out his hand for all of us to shake, even Davy. "Keith asked me to come and show you what's what. This is a bit of an adventure, isn't it?"

"Are you sure it's OK," Jonathan said, "what we're doing? I mean, it's not trespassing or anything, is it?"

Neil gave him what my gran used to call an "old-fashioned look". "Of course it's trespassing," he said. "But don't worry – it's not dangerous. The line isn't electrified – well, not in the sidings, anyway. These tracks haven't been used in years." He leant down to look at Davy, slowly and majestically, like a sort of trainspotter Puddleglum. "You know you must never play on the railway lines, don't you?" he said.

Davy nodded, very serious. "You get squashed," he said. "Strawberry jam!"

"Exactly." Neil looked pleased. "Never play on railway lines. Well. At least, not unless you're with someone who knows what he's doing. Come on."

Behind the station was a big, flat space with a whole mess of railway tracks. It was like a car park for trains. There were a couple of empty carriages parked waiting, and one of those flat-base things they lower shipping containers onto and then hook onto the back of trains. There were also old tracks. Neil was right – they really hadn't been used in years. They were thick with rust, and huge green plants and little saplings sprouted up between the sleepers. And – yes – there was the signal box from the picture. Probably. The windows had been smashed and boarded up, and someone had spray-painted HEX in big black letters across the brickwork. And the tree in the picture was gone. There were some big old buddleia bushes there instead. But . . . yeah . . . it could have been the place in Auntie Irene's photograph.

We lined the photo up with the signal box and the

railway tracks. We guessed that the safe would be buried in about the middle of the photo. Then we turned on the metal detector and began detecting.

We let Davy go first. He swished the detector over the grass and earth in the picture, and whenever it went *beep*, one of us started digging. We dug up quite a lot of rubbish. An old cigarette lighter. Lots of nails. A screwdriver. A spoon. Seventy-five pence in loose change.

And Auntie Irene's safe.

The safe was buried about a foot and a half deep. It looked less like a safe and more like a briefcase, a silvery metal briefcase that might have looked quite swanky if it wasn't covered in earth. It had a handle, and a combination lock. Davy and I tried to open it, but couldn't. Still!

"We did it!" I said. I was so excited. I spun around in little circles of happiness, that's how excited I was. "Look, Jonathan! I was right! It's our treasure!"

"Blimey," said Neil. He looked impressed.

Jonathan just shook his head. He didn't seem to know what to say.

"Are we rich now?" said Davy, hopefully. "Rich enough to buy a bicycle?"

"You bet," I said.

"Mmm," said Jonathan. "Let's see about that."

IN WHICH I CRACK OPEN A SAFE, NINJA-STYLE

We took the safe to the lock-picking class on Wednesday.

"Do you think you'll be able to get in?" I asked Steve, who ran the class. He was a big man with a brown beard that was beginning to go grey and twinkly eyes. He wasn't fat exactly. Just burly.

"All safes are hackable," Steve said. He picked up the briefcase and peered at the combination lock. "They have to be, in case the person who owns it forgets the combination, or something goes wrong with the lock. You need a way in. If nothing else, you can melt it. You know, cut it with a thermic lance or plasma cutters. Or we could blow the lock off. All you need is some nitroglycerine and a battery, pretty much."

"Yeah!" I said. "Let's do that! Where do you buy nitroglycerine from?"

"Well. . ." Steve turned the safe over. "I'm not sure blowing it up or melting it is a good idea. I mean, what's inside? Would it melt? Or burn?"

"It's jewellery," I said. "Would a thermic lance melt jewellery?"

"We don't know it's jewellery," said Jonathan quickly. "It could be anything. Share certificates. Bank statements. Isn't there a less destructive way to get in?"

"Sure," said Steve. "We can drill in. Drill straight through the cam. Although. . ." He frowned at the briefcase. "This is a pretty high-level high-security safe. See, a safe like this, they'll put in cobalt plates to stop you drilling through. Well, you *can* drill through, but you need diamond-tipped drills, and it takes for ever."

"But you can get in?" I said. "Can't you?"

"Oh yes," said Steve. "We'll just drill round it."

As he set up the drill, he explained what he meant. There was a plate of thick metal in front of the lock. But if he drilled down at an angle over the top of the plate, he'd be able to reach the lock. And more importantly, reach the wheels that the combination turned to open the case.

"And then drill through them!"

"Not exactly," said Steve. "Wait and see."

The lock-pickers started coming in as Steve began drilling. Some of them had heard about us and our money. Those people were pretty excited. Jen gave me a big thumbs-up and a grin to show me how pleased she was.

Some of the lock-pickers were all snooty and

pretended to be far too important to care and just sat in their corners, behind their laptops. I bet they cared really.

When he'd finished the drilling, Steve called me over. "OK," he said. He held up an instrument I'd never seen before – a long tube with a handle and an eyepiece at one end. He slotted the tube into the hole and handed me the handle. "Look in there," he said.

I looked into the eyehole. There was a little light shining at the end, and I could see a little row of silvery wheels. "It's a periscope!" I said.

"A borescope," Steve corrected. "Periscopes are for looking around corners. OK, so there's a groove in each of those wheels. And each correct number you put into the combination lines up the groove in one of those wheels. So when you put in the correct combination, all the grooves line up, the bolt slides out and the briefcase opens. Got that?"

"Yup," I said.

"OK," said Steve. "So now it's easy. All you have to do is turn each dial round in turn watching through the borescope. When the groove in the first wheel moves into place, you stop. Then you do the same thing for the next number, and so on until the grooves in all six wheels line up. Simple."

"Cool," said one of the girls who'd come over to listen. That was how you learnt things at the Maker Space. They didn't set you homework or yell at you or anything like that. They just offered you knowledge, and if you wanted it, you took it, and if you didn't, you went and did

89

something else.

Steve made me look through the borescope while he turned the wheels. I'm sure he was just doing it to be nice, because looking and turning are totally multitaskable, but I didn't care. *I cracked a safe! I'm a safe-cracker!* Sizwe would be well impressed.

Maybe if the treasure wasn't in the briefcase, I could get a part-time job as an international jewel thief, I thought. That could work. I could totally lower myself into museums on a wire through the skylight like jewel thieves do.

And then the bolt slid.

And the briefcase opened.

WHAT WAS INSIDE
THE BRIEFCASE ...

. . . was not jewellery.

It was paper. Lots of paper, in clear plastic envelopes.

"That's not treasure!" said Davy. "It's rubbish!"

"Paper can be treasure," said Jen. She picked one of the envelopes out of the box and looked at it. "Whoa. Your aunt was *loaded*."

"What is it?" I asked. The piece of paper didn't make much sense to me. It had the name of some fancy company over the top, and then some numbers – big numbers, thousands of pounds' worth of numbers – underneath. It wasn't a bank statement, though.

"It's a shares certificate," said Jen. "We have some of these for savings." She flicked through the other pieces of paper. "This is a property deed – that's the bit of paper that proves you own your house. Your uncle will be pleased you found that. This is a pension, I think."

"So they're worth money?"

"No," said Jonathan. He took the pieces of paper out of Jen's hand.

"Well. . ." Jen said.

"But shares are money!" I said. "Aren't they – Jen?"

"They're worth money," said Jonathan. "But they don't belong to us. They belonged to our Aunt Irene. And now they belong to Uncle Evan. We'll have to give them back to him. Aunt Irene left us jewellery, Holly. She didn't leave us cash to the value of the jewellery."

"Maybe your uncle—" said Jen.

Jonathan laughed. "Ha!"

I was trying really hard not to cry. Everyone was being so grown-up, and they were treating me like a grown up too. I didn't want to be the little kid who bursts into tears because it's not fair.

But it *wasn't* fair.

It *wasn't*.

UNCLE EVAN

Jonathan sent Uncle Evan an email about the bits of paper, and Uncle Evan rang him up and yelled down the phone at him. I don't know what exactly he said, but Jonathan's side was all "Yes – no – yes, I'm sorry – no, I know I should have – no, we didn't know – yes, of course – yes, but – yes, sorry – I know, but—"

"Isn't he pleased?" I said.

"No," said Jonathan. He looked white and unhappy and most unJonathanlike. "He thinks we're in league with Auntie Irene's ghost or something. He wants to know why we didn't tell him about the photographs straight away. And why we went off to find the treasure without telling him. He thinks we were hoping whatever was in the briefcases was something we could steal."

"What a creep!" I said. "Give me that phone – I'll tell

him! How dare he speak to you like that?"

"Leave it," said Jonathan.

"I mean it!" I said. I wished Mum was here. Mum really hated Uncle Evan. She'd never have let him say things like that.

"Please don't," said Jonathan. "Holly. Don't." He looked utterly miserable. Jonathan hates it when people think badly of him, which is hardly ever, because he usually never does anything interesting enough to offend anyone.

Jo came by after school on Thursday to pick up the bits of paper. I wanted to hold them to ransom, but Jonathan told me I had to give them to her.

"You are a dark horse, aren't you?" said Jo, when I handed her the briefcase.

I scowled. I didn't want praise from people who were stealing the money *we* found.

"Look," said Jo. "I'm really sorry about Dad. I bet he was awful to you. I know you weren't trying to steal anything, really I do."

"Yeah," I said. "Well."

"He wants the photos too," Jo said. She looked at me as though expecting me to fight, but I didn't. After all, maybe Uncle Evan would recognize where the pictures were. Surely, if he found the jewellery, he'd give it to us? Wouldn't he?

"You didn't recognize them, did you?" I asked. She shook her head. "I recognized our living room," she said.

"And the one with the palm trees is Norfolk Island, I'm almost sure. That's in Polynesia – Mum used to have a house out there. She sold the house, though – if she buried anything there, it won't be there now. I don't know about the others."

"OK," I said. I was relieved. Maybe if Jo didn't recognize the photos, Uncle Evan wouldn't either. "And Jonathan's already emailed him the photos. He did it this morning. So."

There was an awkward pause. We were standing on the doorstep because I didn't really want to let her into the flat. I didn't want her to see how messy it was.

"I'm sorry the briefcase didn't have the jewellery in it," she said.

"Do you think—" I said. Jonathan would hate me for asking, but I couldn't *not*. "Do you think Uncle Evan will give us a reward? We found his money, after all. *Loads* of it."

Jo looked uncomfortable.

"No," she said. "I don't think he will. Sorry. But—" She fumbled in her bag for her purse and opened it. She pulled out all the notes she had and handed them to me. "There," she said. "That's to say thank you. It's the least we can do."

"Fifty-five pounds," I told Jonathan. "Fifty-five pounds! There were *thousands* and *thousands* of pounds in that briefcase, and she gave us *fifty-five pounds*! The cheapskate!"

"She shouldn't have given us anything," said Jonathan.

"That money in the briefcase wasn't hers. It's going to go straight to Uncle Evan, remember? Jo didn't get any of it, and I bet he doesn't give her anything either."

That was a good point. I'd forgotten that.

"And actually," Jonathan went on, "she did ring me and say maybe she could give some money, from what her mum left her. But I said no. We *can't* take money from people, Holl. We *can't*."

"You aren't going to give my fifty-five quid back, are you?" I said anxiously.

Jonathan screwed up his face. "I should," he said. "But I can't do that either. I need it to pay the rent."

He looked so unhappy that I put my arms around his waist and hugged him. He looked a bit surprised, but he hugged me back.

"You're a good big brother really," I said.

He patted me on the head. "Good," he said. "Because you're a demon sister from hell."

But I'm pretty sure he meant it as a compliment.

STORIES

We were all miserable that evening. Davy tipped the easy chair in the living room up to make a den, and hid in there with Sebastian. I could hear him in there, whispering secrets into Sebastian's big floppy rabbit ears. I decided to leave him to it.

Jonathan sat behind his computer being miserable and talking to his imaginary internet friends, who live in the pixels. That's what Mum used to call them, anyway, when she wanted to tease him. I didn't want to tease. I'd met some of Jonathan's internet friends. They were real enough.

At about seven o'clock he sat up and said, "This is ridiculous! I'm going to make curry." And he did, an enormous pot of everything-we've-got-in-the-cupboard curry, bananas and peas and tuna fish and leftover cold potatoes and lots and lots of chilli powder. Everyone in our family likes hot curry.

"Tell us a story!" said Davy, when we were all as full as could be.

Jonathan is very good at stories. People don't expect him to be, but he is. He does voices and everything, only not in public. His current story was about Princess Leia and Han Solo, who were going to Mordor to drop the Ring of Power into Mount Doom instead of Frodo and Sam, because Frodo and Sam are OK, but the Millennium Falcon is faster. We were halfway through, but we hadn't had an instalment in ages.

"Why are they sending the Millennium Falcon?" I said. Arguing with Jonathan is an important part of all his stories. "Why can't they just send Superman? It would take him about half a second to get to Mount Doom, and he'd go so fast the Dark Lord would never catch him."

"Superman's in Minas Tirith," said Jonathan. "Fighting the orcs with Gandalf and Dumbledore. And he can't use his super-hearing to hear them, because they've switched the Elven Cloaking Device on in the Millennium Falcon. And they can't turn it off, because if they do the orcs will shoot them down with lasers."

"They should!" said Davy. "They should! They should!" We waited. "They should go in the TARDIS!"

But Jonathan said nobody could Apparate or Disapparate in Mordor, so they couldn't.

Princess Leia and Han Solo were halfway across the Ash Mountains when they got shot down by werewolves with rocket launchers. The werewolves took them to their underground lair, "where Superman can't hear them *either*," because of the built-in soundproof underground-lair layer. And then the werewolves dangled Jar Jar Binks over a pit of molten lava and started lowering him to his death. Something like this always happened to Jar Jar Binks in Jonathan's stories.

"Give us the One Ring or the gungan gets it!" said the head werewolf. But then – *how-woo!* – he fell over dead, because Katniss Everdeen from *The Hunger Games* appeared and shot him in the back of the head with a silver arrow. The werewolves all went after Katniss, and they let go of the rope holding Jar Jar over the pit of molten lava and he plunged to his boiling death, and Davy and I cheered. And then Katniss charged off down the secret passageway, and all the werewolves followed, and she was running fast, but they were running faster, and a chasm opened up in the rock floor, and she leapt over it, but they all leapt after her, and Katniss pulled on a hidden lever handily concealed in a rock formation, and the chasm widened and all the werewolves plunged to their bloody deaths.

Except for this one werewolf. He was at the front of the pack, and his claws scrabbled on the edge of the precipice and he leapt up and onto Katniss. He and Katniss were fighting to the death, teeth and claws, knives and arrows, blood and bones. Princess Leia and Han Solo were watching from the other side of the chasm, but it was too wide for them to jump, and surely,

surely, now all hope was lost.

"Use the Force!" Davy yelled.

"Oh yeah," said Jonathan. "If only one of them thought of that."

And the great wolf pinned Katniss to the ground, and she was struggling, but he was stronger, and he slashed in, all teeth and saliva and mad red eyes. And Leia went, "Oh yeah, the Force!" and she shut her eyes, and the head werewolf dropped dead – hurrah! – and Katniss pulled the lever that shrinks the chasm and leapt back over to say hello to Han and Leia, and they all went back to the underground lair and ate the lasagne that the werewolves were saving for tea. And the next day. . .

"What?" said Davy. "What happened the next day?"

"That," said Jonathan, "is a story for tomorrow."

A WASH-OUT

Several weeks passed and nothing happened. Nobody else commented on our website. I asked Jo to send a link to the page to all her mum's friends, but I don't know if she did. Nobody came forward, anyway.

Social services came up with some money for new school shoes for me and Davy, and a new school bag. Jonathan's social worker said they were still trying to get Jonathan onto the higher level of funding, but the person who needed to approve it had gone off sick, "with stress". People were always going off with stress in social services.

One day, about three weeks after the railway siding, we came into the Maker Space and found Alex in the kitchen, plumbing a new dishwasher into the space where the old one used to sit. The old one was sitting in the doorway, blocking the way in.

"Look what I found!" he said, looking pleased.

"It's a dishwasher," I said. I wasn't that impressed. "So what?"

"So, I found it on Freecycle – it doesn't drain, apparently – the family who owned it just bought a new one. I thought we might see if we can figure out what's wrong with it, and then you guys could take it home with you."

"Seriously?" This was the best news ever. Our own dishwasher. Clean bowls! Never having to scrub mouldy food out of the bottom of a saucepan ever again! "How are you going to fix it?"

Alex shrugged and grinned. "Oh," he said. "Just poke things and see what happens. We can't go too far wrong, right?"

Hmm. Last time Alex said that was when he and Jonathan were trying to fix a telly they found in the street. The telly exploded, set fire to Alex's jacket, and made a perfect smoky black circle on the roof tiles.

Still. A dishwasher! Davy and I kept everything crossed.

SEBASTIAN

Alex and Jonathan brought the dishwasher round on Wednesday evening, in Alex's brother's electrician's van. Then Alex and Jonathan plumbed it in. Then we loaded it with all the bowls and plates with stuck-on baked-bean juice, and knifes and forks with mashed-potato crud still clinging to the edges, and all the glasses with mouldy orange juice on the bottom, and the porridgey bowls that never got cleaned. Then we did a happy soon-to-be-clean-forks dance around the kitchen.

Then Davy and I went to Gran and Grandad's, and Jonathan went to the pub with some school friends who were home from university for the summer.

It was late when we got back. The sun was beginning to set over London, turning the horizon a pale pinky-yellow. It was beginning to drizzle. The street lights glowed yellow in the dark puddles. Davy held my hand and Jonathan's and walked between us, splashing in all the puddles to make the biggest splash he could manage.

"Can we have fish and chips?" he said.

Splash.

"Yeah!" I said. "Chips and lots of vinegar. Davy, stop that, I'm soaking."

"No," said Jonathan. "It's Wednesday – Ranjit shuts early on Wednesdays. And didn't you guys eat already at Gran's house?"

Splash.

"Davy!"

Davy laughed.

"We did," I said. "But we're still hungry. I'm always hungry. Can we have cornflakes?"

"Hey," said Jonathan. "Clean bowls!"

We clomped up the stairs.

"Squelch, squelch, squelch," said Davy.

"It's your own fault," I said.

"*No*," said Davy. "The carpet's all wet."

I pressed my foot down experimentally. Davy was right.

"Oh no," said Jonathan. "Oh no, no, no, no, no."

We opened the door to the flat.

The floor was soaking wet. So was the carpet on the landing. The water wasn't very deep, but there were pizza flyers, and chip packets, and Davy's maths homework flopping wetly in it.

Davy shrieked. "Ew!"

"No," said Jonathan. "No, no, no."

The water ran out over the doorway and began to soak into the stairs. I splashed in on tiptoe, trying to get as little of me wet as possible, and went into the kitchen. That was even wetter.

"The dishwasher's flooded the kitchen!"

I was so disappointed. Our lovely dishwasher! Would the bowls still be clean?

But Jonathan wasn't interested in the bowls. He was more interested in the water. "Get the mop! And the bucket! And – I dunno! Some towels! Quick!"

It took ages to mop up the water and pick out all the bits of wet paper and other stuff that had been lying on the floor. Then Jonathan had to phone Ranjit, and Ranjit said he was coming round to look.

"What's going to happen?" I said. "Have we ruined Ranjit's chip shop? Are we going to have to pay for it to get fixed? We aren't, are we? What if he has to close the shop? Will we have to pay him all the money he would have earned?"

"I don't know," said Jonathan. I must have been making a horribly worried face, because he changed his mind and said, "But he'll have insurance, Holly. He's a sensible grown-up. All sensible grown-ups have insurance."

"But is he insured against us being idiots?" I said, nervously. "What if we do have to pay? We can't afford it, can we?"

Jonathan sighed. "Put Davy to bed, will you?" he said.

"I'm going to see if I can soak up the water on the stairs. And don't *worry*. That's my job."

But I did worry.

Davy went to bed obediently enough, and sat quietly through a chapter of *Beezus and Ramona*, but we were both restless. I tried to read another chapter, but he said, "Shhh."

We could hear Ranjit and Jonathan talking downstairs. Ranjit seemed to be saying a lot. Jonathan didn't seem to be saying much.

After what felt like for ever, I heard the door shut, and Ranjit's feet going downstairs.

I went down. "What did he say?"

Jonathan looked tired, and a little dazed. "He said he's not sure. There's water staining all down the walls, and it's gotten into the electrics, so he's going to have to get someone in to look at it."

"But . . ." I said. "It's insured, isn't it? I mean, we won't have to pay for it?"

Jonathan rubbed his face. "It's not insured against us trying to fix our own dishwasher and then installing it in our kitchen," he said. "And anyway, there's an excess of five hundred pounds on the insurance, Ranjit said."

Five hundred pounds.

"Does that mean we have to pay five hundred pounds?" I said. "It does, doesn't it?"

"I don't know," said Jonathan. "Maybe. It might be more. It might just be some paint. I don't know."

"Social services will give us some money, though, won't they?" I said. "If it's an emergency. They will, won't they?"

"Let's hope so," said Jonathan. He looked shattered. "Please, Holly, just go to bed. I can't think about this right now."

I went to bed, but I couldn't sleep. I tried reading my book. I was reading *The Day of the Triffids*, which is all about how you should never trust plants, because they might turn evil and eat you. But I couldn't concentrate.

We didn't have five hundred pounds. We didn't even have fifty.

It was really early when I woke up. Someone was shaking my arm.

"Holly. *Holly*."

"Davy?"

I opened my eyes.

Davy was standing by the bed in too-small *Doctor Who* pyjamas, holding Sebastian.

"Davy, it's a school day. Can't you go play with your Lego or something?"

"Sebastian's sick."

I sat up, pushing my hair out of my face. I turned my lamp on.

Davy's narrow face appeared, small and worried-looking.

"He's probably just tired, Davy. It's. . ." I looked for my phone, but it was somewhere in the bottom of my school bag. "It's really early. He's probably asleep."

"He's not," said Davy. "He won't move – look." He showed me. Sebastian was lying with his eyes closed. I took him from Davy. He felt warm and heavy, the way he always does, but his heart was beating rapidly beneath my fingers. I bent down and said, "Se-bas-tian. Se-bas-tian," into his ear. I gave him a little gentle shake. Nothing.

"Oh, Davy," I said. *Vets are expensive*, was what I was thinking. *We can't afford this*. But I didn't say it out loud. How could I?

Jonathan took Sebastian to the vet that morning. I thought he wouldn't be able to, because of work, but Davy wouldn't let us leave Sebastian at home, and when we all turned up at the café with a half-dead rabbit, Cath took one look at Sebastian, and at Davy's small mutinous face, and gave Jonathan the morning off. Davy wanted to go too, but Jonathan said he had to go to school.

"Don't let them kill him without me!" said Davy fiercely. "I'll never forgive you if you do! *Never!*" I don't think I'd ever seen him this fierce about anything before.

Jonathan got an early emergency appointment, as soon as the surgery opened. I rang him up at break time to find out what had happened.

"He's got. . ." he said. He hesitated. "Well, I'm not sure exactly what it is. Something complicated. They did explain. Some sort of tumour, but one they can deal with. They can cut it out, they said, but then there are injections and things as well." He sounded worried.

"Oh," I said. I was in our house block, and it was pretty noisy. Behind me three kids were having a yoghurt fight, and the teacher was yelling at them to stop. "But they can fix it?"

"Yes," said Jonathan. "I think so. It sounded like they could. But, Holly, it's expensive. Like, hundreds of pounds' worth of expensive. Probably more. I'm not entirely sure how much more. I got depressed and stopped listening once it got into the hundreds. The operation's one thing, but you have to keep buying the drugs for ages afterwards. Even if we could afford the operation, to start with. Which we can't."

"We could ask social services?" I said hopefully.

"Yeah," said Jonathan. "And I will. Of course I will. But I'm already asking them about the dishwasher. And school shoes are one thing, but when you're asking for money for something that's your fault – which the dishwasher is, really – they – well, they get sniffy. And pets aren't exactly an emergency, are they?"

"Yes, they are!" I said. "They're an emergency for Davy! You have to tell them! You have to make them see!"

"I know," said Jonathan. "I'll try. Just. . ."

"Just what?" I said, but he didn't reply.

"WHAT DO YOU WANT ME TO DO?"

I didn't tell Davy what was wrong with Sebastian when I picked him up from school. I didn't know how. I also didn't really know what was going to happen next. I mean, maybe we could get the money from somewhere. Right? We could sell Jonathan's computer. Or all Davy's Lego. Or . . . there must be lots of ways to earn money. We could go bag-packing in Tesco, like the Scouts do. Or carol-singing. I mean, it was July, so obviously not carols, but busking. Or we could ask everyone who commented on my blog to give us money or. . .

"No," said Jonathan.

"We can't put Sebastian down," I said.

"What do you want me to do?" said Jonathan. "Honestly, Holly, tell me. What? Have you got a thousand pounds hidden in your knicker drawer? Because I haven't."

"Maybe social services'll give us extra money,"
I said. "Or maybe they'll hurry up and give you the
higher-level foster-care allowance if they know how
urgent it is."

"Maybe," said Jonathan. He didn't sound convinced.

"Or," I said, "we could go and find the rest of Auntie
Irene's treasure."

Jonathan sighed. "Holly. . ."

"We should! There's lots of things we could do! We
could ring up everyone in her address book and see if
they know where those places are! We could bribe her
secretary! We could!"

"She didn't have a secretary! She was retired! We
don't even know for sure that she *did* hide anything in
any of those places—"

"Auntie Irene wouldn't have given those photographs
to me if she didn't think they'd be useful," I said,
stubbornly. Jonathan gave me a frustrated look.

"She'd had a stroke," he said. "Who knows what she
thought she was doing. Maybe she thought she was giving
you the GPS coordinates at the same time. Who knows?"

I wanted to punch him. I wanted to scream. "You
don't care about Sebastian!" I yelled. "You don't care
about any of us!"

"Fine," said Jonathan. "Right. Yes. I don't care. Now,
can I go upstairs now, please? I've got to go and tell Davy
we can't afford to cure his rabbit."

And then I felt bad. Because I knew what I'd said
wasn't true. So then I felt even worse than I had before.

*

Davy was horribly upset about Sebastian. I knew he would be, but I hadn't realized quite how much. He didn't argue, Jonathan said. He just sat there. And then he climbed into bed and pulled the duvet over his head and wouldn't speak to either of us all evening.

Jonathan called his social worker, Philip-the-dull. He shut himself in the living room, but I listened at the door.

"Yes—" Jonathan said. "Yes, I know – yes, but how long? Because this is really urgent. . . No, not the floor. The rabbit. Yes, I know it's only a rabbit. . . Yes. Yes, no, I understand. But this is important. It's more important than school trips. . . No, no, I do understand that. Yes, I know education is important. I know. But— Well, I'm sorry, but I don't care about your funding cuts! . . . No, *you* calm down! I don't think I've got anything to be calm about, do *you*?" And he slammed the phone down, hard.

I put my head round the door. "Well?" I said.

"Rabbits are not an emergency," said Jonathan. He'd flushed up bright red. "*Apparently*. And Philip doesn't know when we'll get our extra money, but not for weeks yet. He thinks he'll be able to wangle something for the floor, though. Like anyone cares about *that*!"

I woke up in the middle of the night, and couldn't get back to sleep. I was so scared. I was scared of not having money all the time. I was scared of how long we could go on like this, when something tiny going wrong meant we couldn't pay the rent, and what would happen if we couldn't pay the rent? Would social services help us out? Or would we have to move house? Leave everything behind? Granny and Grandad. The Maker Space. Sizwe and Neema, and Jen teaching me how to program, and our lovely little flat with the trains rattling past the windows in the night, and my bedroom wallpaper with stars on it that Mum helped me pick out and put up for me, and the door to our flat that she painted fire-engine red and . . . I wanted to cry. I hardly *ever* cry, but I wanted to now. I went downstairs.

Jonathan was sitting on one of the comfy chairs in the living room, on his computer. The room was dark. The only light was coming from the computer screen.

"Jonathan?" I said.

He looked round. "Holly? Are you all right?"

"We aren't really going to put Sebastian down, are we?" I said.

Jonathan sighed. "I don't know," he said. "I'm sorry, Holly. I really don't know what else to do."

"We can't go on like this," I said. "Can we? Not having enough money all the time. You're going to have to do something about it, aren't you? What are you going to do? What if social services never give you the extra money? Are you going to send me and Davy off to New Zealand?"

"No!" Jonathan looked really shocked. "Holly. No. Of course not. Unless – I mean, unless you'd rather. You'd have proper clothes and food and stuff over there, you know. And there's mountains and things."

I sat on the edge of the sofa and leant against him.

"Silly Jonathan," I said. "You know we wouldn't rather."

Jonathan nodded. "All right," he said. "Please don't worry, Holly. I'll figure something out."

But I couldn't see what.

SCIENCE SOLVES EVERYTHING

We were still in an awful mood on Sunday, when we went to the Maker Space.

Jen waved at us, and wandered over. "Hey, Davy-face," she said, holding out her hand.

Davy wouldn't even look at her. He ran over to one of the chairs and curled into a little ball, with his face pressed up against the wall.

Jen gave me a questioning look, so I explained about Sebastian. "And if I could just find Auntie Irene's treasure, everything would be all right. But I don't know *how*!" I said. "Nobody knows where any of the photos are! I've asked everyone I know. There must be a better way to find where they are. There must. But I just *can't think*!" I flopped down on the chair next to Jen, crossed my arms over my stomach, and groaned. Loudly. "Aren't there techy things you could do? Like, image-recognition software or something?"

"Hmm." Jen sounded doubtful. "The thing is, for image-recognition software to work, there need to be other images to compare the pictures to. I mean—" She brought up my blog and tapped the photograph of Auntie Irene's living-room wall. "If the internet was full of pictures of your aunt's living room, I'm sure it would be pretty easy to identify this one. But it's not going to be, is it? And the same with these beaches and stuff. It's not like they're Blackpool Pier." She scrolled down to the grey little beach. "Look at this. It's just a bit of coast. It's going to be a pretty remote bit too if your aunt buried treasure there, isn't it? And even if there *are* pictures of this place online, there must be hundreds of beaches that look a bit like this."

"I suppose so." I leant over her chair so I could see the picture. I'd stared at the photographs so often, I bet I could have picked those rocks out of a rock line-up.

"It's a shame your aunt didn't have a digital camera," Jen said. "There are all sorts of things you can do with a digital photo. You can look up the metadata, for example – that's often got the latitude and longitude in there. But—"

"Oooh!" I said. "Ooh, Jen!" Because Auntie Irene *did* have a digital camera. In fact, she had several. She *loved* technology. She was the first person I knew to get a smartphone. Mum told me she'd only found out what a digital camera *was* when Aunt Irene showed up with one.

That evening, when we got home, I called Jo. "Do you know where your mum kept her digital photos?"

"Not sure," said Jo. "Why?"

"It's about us finding the rest of the treasure," I said. "Yours and ours. I was thinking, if I could see the digital copies of the photos she gave me, it might help tell us where they were taken. Metadata and stuff," I said airily. "You know."

"I don't know for sure," said Jo. "But I did take her laptop for Noah. Don't tell Dad. I was so annoyed – with Mum for making everything so complicated and with him for not sticking up for us. The boys wanted a laptop, and it's not as though he was ever going to use it. It won't be much use to you, though – all her files are password-protected."

I smiled, although Jo couldn't see that, of course. It was my special, *I am a computer genius and so is my brother so let me get the mission codes for you* smile. Passwords? Ha!

"Passwords," I said, "will not be a problem."

CHILD HACKER SOLVES CASE. POLICE MARVEL.

Jo came round with the computer after school on Monday. I'd meant to meet her on the doorstep as usual, because the flat's always such a mess, but I was upstairs trying to actually do some English homework, and Davy buzzed the intercom before I could get down. She didn't say anything, but the kitchen smelt of slightly rotten milk and wet carpet from the overflowing dishwasher and the bin was overflowing in a disgusting sort of way, and there was a stain on the hall carpet, where Davy had spilt honey that morning and no one had bothered to clean it up, and I could see the unhappy way her face tightened.

"Are you all right, Holly?" she said, her head making small, anxious twitches. "Looking after Davy on your own? I feel like I ought to help more than I do, but it's so difficult, with the business, and the boys—"

"We're fine," I said. I was beginning to see what Jonathan meant about asking too much of people. I liked being taken out for cake, and getting new video games for Christmas, and Auntie Irene's laptop, which she said I didn't need to worry about giving back, actually, and I didn't want to ruin that by asking for help.

"If there's anything I can do," she said awkwardly.

Adopt us, I wanted to say. *Let us come and live in your nice house, and Davy go to your childminder, and Jonathan go to university, and everything be like it was when Mum was alive.*

But I didn't, of course. You can't just ask people to adopt you. Not even nice ones.

Auntie Irene's laptop was stupidly easy to hack into. I just unattached the hard drive and plugged it into Jonathan's laptop. It whirred for a bit, and then all the files Auntie Irene had saved onto it flashed up on screen. Easy.

"Now what?" said Davy, who was watching with interest.

"Now I need to find her pictures. If they're on here. Which they might not be."

I was pretty worried about this, actually. Auntie Irene certainly wasn't the sort of person who would leave important information lying around. Would she just leave the pictures on her laptop? Wouldn't she make copies of them and hide them . . . somewhere?

I spent the afternoon looking through all her files.

Files and files of pictures. Baby pictures of Jo. Holiday pictures. There were even a couple of pictures of us, at family parties.

Then there were folders and folders of really boring pictures. Landscapes. People in suits. Pictures of the inside of engines, and circuit-board designs. Folders and folders of machine parts, all neatly labelled.

Auntie Irene was *weird*.

I looked through every picture on her computer. Nothing. I ran a search for all the sorts of image files I knew and found a whole lot that weren't saved under pictures, but none of them were the pictures in Auntie Irene's album.

I called Jen. She was at work, but she answered anyway.

"I can't *find* them," I wailed.

Jen sighed. "She might not have kept copies," she said gently.

But I was in no mood for gentleness. "There's no way she *wouldn't*," I said. "She was super-organized. She wouldn't just have one photo album that might get lost down the back of the sofa. She'd have that information in *loads* of places. Where else might she have put it? Where would she have hid them? Her phone? The internet?"

"Anywhere," said Jen. "Her knicker drawer?" Which *wasn't helpful*.

I told her so. I could hear her smiling at me down the phone.

"Maybe some sort of online file storage?" she suggested.

"How would I know if she had?" I said.

"I dunno. Look in her history?"

I felt really weird going through Auntie Irene's internet history. Like I was watching her undress or something. I wondered if I was going to discover loads of dark secrets. But I didn't. I hadn't heard of most of the websites she used to visit, apart from the obvious ones like Google, or Waitrose, or the BBC news website.

"What should I be looking for?" I asked Jen.

"Well, there are lots of file-sharing websites," Jen said. "Look for something that describes itself as a cloud, or file storage or file sharing or backup or something."

I kept looking. And then.

"I found it! Online file sharing and backup software! This is it!"

"So click through," said Jen.

I did. The link went straight through to the login page. The login page had two boxes for username and password. And both the boxes had that little line of stars which meant that you'd asked the website to store your password for you. I clicked on the button that said Log in.

And there I was.

There was a whole page of different files, with names that were mostly numbers. And some folders. And one folder called Briefcases.

I opened the folder.

And there they were.

All five pictures.

"Jen!" I squealed. "Jen, they're here! I found them! What do I do now?"

"Click on a picture!" said Jen. I clicked on the first picture, the Polynesian one. Pale blue sea the colour of hotel swimming pools, and hope, and money. Pale, clean sand. A blue sky with no worries in it. "And look in . . . properties, I think?"

I right-clicked the picture, and then clicked on Properties. A dialogue box came up with three tags. I clicked on Metadata.

The Metadata tab was this list of information about Auntie Irene's photographs. Most of them were really boring stuff like Aperture Value and Exposure Length. Some of the spaces where properties should have been were blank. But there, about halfway down, was a space marked Location.

"There's a number!" I said. "But what does it *mean*?"

"It's the latitude and longitude," said Jen. "Hang on, there must be a website that tells you where that is. Let me have a look." There was a pause. "OK. Got one. Type 'latitude and longitude' into Google and click on the first link. There's a space at the bottom where you can type in the coordinates."

I did as she said. The map page came up with a picture of a piece of coastline, with one of those little pointer things stuck onto it. It could have been anywhere. I zoomed out, trying to find a picture that was small enough to see where it was.

"Norfolk Island! That's right! That's where Jo said it was! Polynesia!"

"Polynesia," said Jen. She laughed. "Well, good luck

with that one, Holly."

Yeah, yeah. But. . .

I clicked back onto the tab with the metadata.

"Here!" I said to Jen. "Under Date/Time! It says this picture was taken four years ago. Well, Jo saw the jewellery two years ago, so she can't have hidden it here. We just need to look at the date the photo was taken, and I bet we'll be able to rule loads of them out!"

Jonathan would have told me not to get so excited before anything had actually happened. But Jen sounded as thrilled as I was. "Go on, then!" she said. "Get looking. . ."

I opened the other pictures. The dates were all different. Auntie Irene's living room was the oldest one. Then the Norfolk Island picture. Then the railway siding. That one was three years old. If we'd known that at the time, we could have saved ourselves a journey.

There were only two pictures that had been taken in the last two years. One was the messy office. The other was the one of the little beach. Grey rocks, grey sea, grey sky and long grass and heavy clouds.

The messy office was in a building called Conway Place. It was in London, near Angel. From the photograph, it looked like a big old five-storey house. I told Jen the postcode, and we both put it into Google. The postcode came up with the websites of lots of different companies who had offices there.

"This office could belong to any of these people!" I said.

"This place is huge! Do we have to check every office?"

"Nope," said Jen. "Put 'Irene Kennet, Conway Place' into Google. First hit."

I did as she told me. The first hit was the website of a company called Inspired Solutions. They'd apparently designed a new type of wire. Their website said they were a *small, dynamic organization with big ambitions!* There was a whole lot of guff about their wire, which sounded dead boring, and then at the bottom, it said, *With many thanks to our sponsors and supporters*, and there was a long list of people, including Auntie Irene.

"There you go," said Jen. "What about this beach?"

I copied the latitude and longitude into the latitude and longitude website and waited. It came up with an aerial photograph of some patchwork fields in various shades of green and yellow and brown, some tiny toy houses, a rocky coastline, blue sea. I zoomed out.

"Papa Westray – it's another island!"

Jen laughed. "Did your aunt like islands?" she said.

"I don't know," I said. "But I do. I love them! Islands are my favourite thing!"

Jen laughed again. "Where is this island, then?" she said.

I zoomed out again. The picture shrank and shrank. Westray. Orkney. Scotland.

"It's in Scotland! Right at the top of Scotland!" I gave a little bounce in my seat. "We could go to both those places! We really, really could!"

SIZWE'S MUM

I decided, on reflection, not to tell Jonathan about the office. Breaking into someone else's workplace and stealing their briefcase was the sort of thing that would only worry him. Far better to deal with this problem myself. Sizwe and Neema, I decided, were much better accomplices.

I told them all about it at break time the next day.

"OK," said Neema. "Cool. What are you going to do? Go to the office and ask if your auntie left any briefcases lying around?"

"I dunno," I said. I'd been thinking about this. "Won't they just say no? I mean, even if they were hiding Auntie Irene's briefcase for her – they were *hiding* it, weren't they? They aren't going to give it to us. Sherlock Holmes wouldn't just go and ask. He'd disguise himself as a workman and spend all day tapping the walls pretending he was looking for dry rot until he'd found the secret hiding place. And Lord Peter would send one of his ninja typists in to suss the place out after everyone had gone home. I think that's what we ought to do. But you have to be a grown-up to disguise yourself – it doesn't work if you're a kid."

(Lord Peter Wimsey was another old-fashioned detective I liked. He was like Sherlock Holmes, but posher and funnier. He had this typing agency full of respectable-looking old ladies, who he'd secretly trained in lock-picking and surveillance and asking questions, and whenever he had a mission like this one, he'd send one of them in, in disguise.)

Neema and Sizwe had never heard of Lord Peter and his undercover typists, though (they'd only heard of Sherlock Holmes because of Benedict Cumberbatch), so I had to explain.

I was halfway through my explanation when Sizwe started bouncing up and down and waving his hands about. "I know!" he said. "I know what we've got to do! I've got the perfect plan!"

"What?" I said, but Sizwe had already taken his phone out and was looking up the phone number of Inspired Solutions. He made flappy "shh" motions at me.

Then he dialled. "Hullo? . . . Hullo, yes, I'm doing a school project on cleaners. Like, do businesses use big cleaning firms, or hire people themselves, or what? . . . Yeah, it's business studies. . . Oh, OK. . . Yeah, could you give me the name of the company, please? I'm supposed to do a graph. . . Yeah, no problem. . . OK. Thanks! Bye." He put down the phone and grinned at me. "I'm good," he said. "Tell me I'm good."

"You're baffling," I said. "Are you going to pretend to be a cleaner?"

"No," he said. "I'm going to get my mum to pretend to be a cleaner. Well, not pretend. Actually be. And then I'm going to go with her – that's totally allowed, I used to do that all the time when I was little. " He caught Neema's puzzled expression. "My mum runs a cleaning firm," he explained. "And, see, look, I asked the lady on the phone who their cleaners are. It's this firm called Speedy Brooms. And my mum knows them! Well, she knows the lady who runs them. I bet she could persuade them to let her go in and do the cleaning instead of whoever it is who's supposed to do it. They do that – take over each other's shifts when people go on holiday and stuff. And I could come too! And then we'd find out what's what."

THE OFFICE

The next day, I took our broom-handle metal detector to school and gave it to Sizwe. The other kids thought we were crazy.

"What's *that* for?" Kali said.

"We's gonna catch us a wabbit!" said Sizwe.

"Huh?" said Kali.

Sizwe tapped his nose mysteriously.

Sizwe called me up that evening. "OK," he said. "So Mum and I went in, and it's totally the right office. I mean, it looked exactly like that picture. I took a photo to prove it – I'll send it over when I'm off the phone."

(He did. He was right. The office in his photograph *did* look like the one Auntie Irene had given me.)

"So," Sizwe went on, "we went up, and I had the

metal detector like you said, only it was pretty useless because loads of stuff in an office is made of metal, isn't it? I mean, even the tables were, so it just detected everything, and then a cross man in a suit told me to shut it up, so I had to. But I found a nice lady called Sue who worked in admin, and I asked her about your Auntie Irene, and they said she used to work there, but hadn't for years. Six years ago, she left, they said."

"Yeah, but she must have been back," I said. "That photograph was taken two years ago."

"I *know*," said Sizwe. "Stop interrupting, woman. I *told* them that. Well, I didn't. I said I thought my friend's auntie had been back since then, and had she? And Sue said yes, she had, she'd come back a couple of times to do consulting work. But she'd definitely retired, because last time she came, she'd taken all her stuff with her. So I said, what stuff? And she said – guess what she said?"

"A briefcase!"

"Yes! And I said, oh, had you been keeping a briefcase hidden for her then? All casual, and Sherlock Holmes-like. And *she* laughed a bit and said, oh yeah, Irene had left all sorts of stuff clogging up their safe. So I went and had a look. It was just an ordinary safe, only it was sort of built into the wall. It looked really properly ancient. Sue said nobody knew what the combination was, but the lock *did* turn, which is weird when you think about it, isn't it? I mean, you'd expect a really ancient safe with a really ancient lock that hadn't been opened in years to sort of be rusted shut, wouldn't you? So *I* think she fixed the safe, or found the combination, or got a locksmith in to sort it out, or something, while she worked there. And that that's where the briefcase was!"

"But it's gone," I said.

"Yeah," said Sizwe. "But that's good, isn't it? That means the jewellery can't have been hidden in that briefcase. Because one of those photographs must be of the place where she hid the jewellery, mustn't it? Otherwise what would be the point of giving them to you? And if there isn't a briefcase in that office any more, then that can't have been the photograph you wanted, can it? So now you know where the jewellery is. Don't you? It's in Orkney. It's the only place left it could be."

NO

"No," said Jonathan. "That's all. No."

"Yes!" I said. "Yes, yes, yes, yes, yes!"

"Holly, don't," he said. "Just don't. Think about it! Train tickets to Scotland! Boats, and . . . taxis, and . . . I don't know. Hotel rooms! Food! How am I supposed to afford all of that?"

"By finding the treasure!" I wailed. "It'll solve everything!"

"Yeah," said Jonathan. "Like last time."

I started to cry. I couldn't help it.

Jonathan sighed. "Look," he said. "I'm sorry. But there's no way you can know for sure that Auntie Irene's treasure is in that briefcase. She'd had a stroke! She could have been completely batty, for all you know! I'm not wasting what money we have on going all the way up to Scotland on a wild goose chase."

"I hate you!" I said. "You don't care about Sebastian at all!"

I ran upstairs and wrote a long and angry blog post all about Jonathan. Then I deleted it without posting. Jonathan's all right. Even if he is an idiot.

I called Jen instead and told her about it. Jen is a great listener. She kept quiet all the time I was talking, then she said, "How much money would you need?"

"I don't know," I said. "It's in Orkney, which is right at the top of Scotland. There's a train journey, then a ferry, then a bus, then another ferry, then another ferry. I looked it up. It takes ages. We'd need places to stay, and money, and . . . I dunno. Maybe Jonathan's right."

"Wait there," said Jen. And she put the phone down.

I waited.

Davy came and knocked on my door. "Jonathan's shut himself in his room and he won't let me in," he said. "Is there dinner?"

"I dunno," I said. "Shall we see?"

We went and looked in the kitchen.

"What do you want?"

"Eggs and fried potatoes."

"I don't know how to do fried potatoes." That was one of Jonathan's recipes. "I can do boiled."

I made scrambled eggs and boiled potatoes for Davy. They didn't taste as nice as Jonathan's potatoes, but we covered them in tomato ketchup, and they tasted OK. Jonathan came down and ate with us, but he didn't say much. We watched *Despicable Me* and pretended like everything was all right. Jonathan went upstairs before the film had finished. He looked as though he'd been crying. I wondered if he had.

LIFE IS AN ADVENTURE

Gran rang just after Davy had gone to bed. I told her about the photographs, and the treasure in Orkney. She was like Jen – a brilliant person to tell.

"Oh, my dear," she said. "The Orkney Islands! One of my favourite places in the whole world."

"Are they?" I said. This was the first I'd heard of it. "What are they like?"

"Old," she said, after thinking about it for a moment. "They have villages there that were old when the Vikings came. Fairy hills, and standing stones and the tombs of kings. And really excellent fudge."

"Really?" I said.

"Two of my dearest friends live there," she said. "Derek and Shirley. They live on the tiniest little island. Derek was the island postman, policeman and taxi driver.

And Shirley was fireman, barkeep and driver of the school boat. I expect you'll need somewhere to stay when you get there," she went on. "Let me know when you're going and I'll tell Derek to expect you."

"We're not going, Gran," I said sadly. "Jonathan thinks it's too far and too expensive."

"Oh, my dear," said Gran. "I love Jonathan very much, but you tell him from me, life is an adventure. And there's only one way to have an adventure – or a life, I suppose – and that's just to do it."

"I'll tell him," I said. "Thanks, Gran."

But I was fairly sure he wouldn't listen.

MIRACLES AND WONDERS

I was cleaning my teeth when Jen rang back.

"OK," she said. "I've spoken to Keith. He put a thing out on his mailing group, and he's found a friend who has a bunch of complimentary rail vouchers which he got because he and his kids were on a long-distance train from London to Penzance which got delayed by three hours because the line got flooded, and then all the lights went out in his carriage, and the power sockets stopped working, and the café ran out of tea. But they were only valid for six months, and they're about to expire, and he hasn't used all of them, so he said you could have them."

"Seriously?" I said.

"And," said Jen, "Keith has a friend who works at King's Cross, who says if you go down there and ask for him, he'll tell you what the best trains are to get, and

143

make sure Davy and Jonathan are in the same cabin together on the sleeper train – Keith thinks the sleeper train is the best one to get coming back, and I think he's right, sleeper trains are awesome."

"Totally awesome," I said. I meant it. I was feeling a bit dazed.

"I put a thing out on the Maker Space mailing list," Jen went on. "You'll need someone to stay with on the way up. Because I know Jonathan can't miss many days of work, so I thought you'd probably want to go on a Friday after school, right? I mean, if Jonathan can get time off work. And then you'll miss the last ferry. So, anyway, depending on what train you get, there are lots of places you could stay that are sort of halfway between here and there. A couple of people from the Maker Space in Newcastle said you could stay with them, but I don't know who either of them is, so wait if you want to stay in Newcastle and I'll check them out. I also know someone in Glasgow, but she's a bit grumpy, and Natalie Hollis has a friend in Aberdeen she thinks will probably let you stay, so there'll definitely be someone, so find out from Jonathan what he'd like to do and let me know, OK?"

"OK," I said. "Um—"

"I don't know what you're going to do when you get to Orkney, though," Jen said. "I did ask if anyone knew anyone in Orkney, but nobody seemed to. I thought I might put out a thing on Facebook maybe, but I wanted to check with you first if that would be OK. I thought if the worst came to the worst you could camp? We've got an only-slightly-leaky tent you could borrow."

"It's all right," I said. "Gran knows someone in Orkney we can stay with. She already said we could."

"Oh," said Jen. "Right. Good. Now, you'll have to pay for ferries and buses and things – is that OK? If it's not – I dunno, maybe we could do a whip-round?"

I blinked.

She waited.

"I'll ask," I said. I poked my head round the living-room door, where Jonathan was on his laptop on the sofa. *Obviously* eavesdropping.

"Do we have enough money to pay for ferries and buses?" I asked. "Because someone Keith knows is going to give us magic train tickets, and Jen's found someone we can stay with in Aberdeen and we can go up on Friday night after school, she says, so you only have to miss work on Saturday and Monday, and do we want a collection? We could spend it on haggis. I've never had haggis."

Jonathan looked like I'd just thrown his hard drive into a pit of lava.

I handed him the phone.

"Now, look—" I heard Jen say. Then there was a lot of talking. Jonathan said, "But what about—" and "But I can't—" and "But I couldn't—" Then he shut up and just made squeaky, grunty, groany noises. Then he stopped making even those and just sat there shaking his head.

Then he said, "Actually, we've still go some overdraft

left. I was saving it for frivolities like dentist's bills."

Then he said, "Is Natalie's friend called Kate? Because I know her. We'll stay with her."

Then he said, "Thank you. It's really very – thank you."

Then he put the phone down.

ACTUALLY ACTUAL

"I don't have much choice really, do I?" said Jonathan grumpily. But he looked a bit pleased, I thought.

"It's a holiday!" I said. "To a foreign country! It'll be wonderful! There'll be bagpipes! And haggis! And kilts! And the Loch Ness monster! Oh, Jonathan, please don't look like that. Aren't you even a little bit excited?"

"Maybe a bit," said Jonathan. He looked at me. Then he did something he hardly ever does. He put his arm around me and gave me a squeeze. "But if it all goes wrong, I'm blaming you, OK?"

Jonathan and I worked out the plan. Well, Jonathan did really, but I watched. Jonathan would leave work early, collect us both from school and we'd get the train to Aberdeen, stay the night with Natalie's friend Kate, then get a ferry-bus-ferry-ferry to the island with the beach with the treasure. We'd bring a tent for the first night on the mainland, which was what the biggest Orkney island was called, and then stay with Gran's friends on Papa Westray the second night. We had the tent we used to use for camping holidays when Mum was alive, so that was all right. Then we'd spend a day finding whatever it was that Auntie Irene had hidden in her safe, and then get the sleeper train home on Monday night. That way, Jonathan would only have to miss two days of work, and Davy and I would miss one day of school.

"So, who is this Kate person?" I asked Jonathan. "Do you know her?"

Jonathan went red. "Well . . ." he said. "Sort of. She's . . . I know her online. A bit."

"Is she the person you're always talking to online?" I asked. "She is! Is she your internet girlfriend?"

"No." Jonathan went even redder. "Shut up. She's just . . . someone I know, that's all."

"I bet she's fifty and bald in real life," I told him.

But he said Alex had met her, and she wasn't.

Jonathan wasn't at all sure we should bring Davy.

"He's expensive," he said. "Extra tickets for everywhere. And late nights, and sleeping in tents, and not knowing what we're going to find when we get there. He could stay with Gran, maybe, like Sebastian is?"

The vet had given Sebastian an injection, which had stopped him lying there in that awful, half-dead way.

But he still didn't look very happy. We'd left him with Gran and half a value pack of carrots. Davy had originally wanted Sebastian to come to Orkney too, but even I thought that was a bad idea.

"No!" said Davy. He folded his arms and glared at Jonathan.

"No," I said. There was only one step from "let's leave Davy behind" to "let's leave Holly behind", and I wasn't having that. This was our quest. It belonged to us.

Jonathan knew that, I think. He didn't argue, anyway. He folded his arms – just like Davy – and leant against the wall, and sighed. "Seven hours!" he said. "Seven hours on a train with a seven year old! And then a ferry! Three ferries! And then back! I must be mad! Are you sure you wouldn't rather stay with Gran, Davy?"

"No," said Davy, again. "I'm coming too. So don't try and stop me!"

HERE WE COME

Really, it should be me whose job it is to look after our family. I do it way better than Jonathan does. I did all the packing for me and Davy. Jonathan just packed the tent and camping stuff, and an overnight bag. I packed:

All the scrap paper from the scrap-paper box.

Felt-tip pens.

All eight Harry Potter DVDs, and headphones.

Three books for me and two for Davy.

Travel Scrabble and Uno and a pack of cards.

Food. You can buy food on trains, but it's expensive, so we brought our own. We brought a loaf of bread, and a packet of cheese, and a penknife and three apples and three bananas and a packet of chocolate biscuits. And two bottles of orange squash. The bananas got a bit crushed, but the rest of the food was OK.

Actually, the whole journey was OK. Keith's railway friend at King's Cross was brilliant. "Orkney, eh?" he said, as we handed over the vouchers Keith had given us and he set about printing our tickets. "Good-oh."

We had a table, which we shared with a grumpy businessman, who looked a bit annoyed when we brought out the Scrabble board. But after Darlington, he got replaced by a friendly lady, who thought the whole thing was very exciting, and played Shop Snap with me and Davy all the way to Newcastle. And then Jonathan and Davy watched *Harry Potter* with one headphone each, and I read *A Study in Scarlet*. And after a while I got too tired to read, so I just sat in my seat and looked out of the window and . . . wondered.

ABERDEEN

It was late when we got to Aberdeen. Kate, Jonathan's mysterious internet girlfriend, had given us directions, which involved a bus and then a walk through the dark streets. It was hard to tell what Aberdeen was really like. Dark. Tall buildings. Fresher air than London. And all the people on the bus had Scottish accents, which was strange and exciting.

"How much *further?*" said Davy. Davy was so tired he was nearly falling over. I was tired too. And hungry.

"Not far," said Jonathan, but he looked worried. He had his *am I being a proper grown up?* face on. The one he wears when we have cheese sandwiches for tea three nights in a row.

Kate lived in a little flat in a tenement building, just like the poor kids did in *Greyfriars Bobby*. It looked like what you'd imagine a Victorian block of flats would look like. Tall and rectangular and made out of dirty grey stone.

Jonathan rang the bell, and this girl answered. She looked at Jonathan and burst out laughing. Jonathan looked hurt.

"I'm sorry," said the girl. "I really am. Don't look like that! But just—" She tried to catch her breath, but it got lost in something somewhere between a hiccup and a giggle. "Just look at us!"

I looked at the girl, and then I looked at Jonathan. Jonathan gave a reluctant sort of half-smile. Then he giggled too.

"What?" said Davy. "What's so funny? I don't get it!"

I did. The girl – Kate – looked like a female version of Jonathan. She was tall and skinny and dressed in blue jeans with holes in the knee, and a hoodie that said Aberdeen University Quidditch Team. She had yellowy-red hair. I wondered if it was auburn, like Anne's in *Anne of Green Gables*, but she told me later it was strawberry blonde. She had pale skin, not creepy-vampire pale, more like a china doll. She had freckles all across her nose. She was laughing.

"Hello," she said, and she stuck out her hand. "I'm Kate. I know you're Jonathan." She made an expression of exaggerated surprise at Davy and me. "And you're Holly and Davy, right?"

"Yeah," I said. "Weren't you expecting us?"

"Oh yes," Kate said cheerfully. "I just didn't realize you were kids, that's all. I thought you were grown-ups."

"Didn't you read our website?" I said, and she said she hadn't.

I started to explain, but she stopped me and said, "Davy looks like he's about to fall asleep on his feet. Shall we eat?"

We'd already eaten cheese sandwiches on the train, but we were still hungry. Kate had made a sort of pasta thing with cheese and mushrooms and peppers and chunks of sausage. It was amazing. I told her so. "This is so good. Is it hard to make?"

"It mostly came out of a jar," Kate whispered. "The sauce did, anyway. But don't tell, OK?"

But I totally am. If food in jars is this good, Jonathan should buy it, and then we wouldn't have to eat so many jacket potatoes and peanut-butter sandwiches.

Kate was right about Davy. Even the cheesy sausage pasta wasn't enough to keep him awake. He was nearly falling over into his bowl. In the end, Jonathan took him off to clean his teeth and go to bed. Jonathan and Davy were sleeping in Kate's flatmate's bed, because Kate's flatmate had gone home for the summer holidays. I was on the fold-out sofa in the living room.

When Jonathan had gone, Kate said, "OK. Spill. What exactly's going on?"

So I told her all about Jonathan and Auntie Irene and the treasure and Sebastian, and the wonderful way everyone seemed to want to help us. "Didn't you know about this?" I said. "I thought you and Jonathan were friends." And Kate explained that they were friends in a reading-each-other's-stories-and-sharing-funny-stuff sort of way, and that she'd known that Jonathan lived in London and worked in a café, but she hadn't known about Mum, or us, or why he wasn't at university.

"The internet's not like that," she said. "You share the stuff you want to share, and you keep the rest quiet."

"But how can you be friends if you don't know stuff like that?" I asked, and Kate shrugged.

"Do your friends know everything about you?" she said, which shut me up. Nobody knows everything about me. Even you, reading this book, even you don't know everything.

"The thing I don't understand," said Kate, as Jonathan came back, "is, if your mum was in the police and Jonathan's a waiter, then – no offence – but how do you earn enough money to pay the rent? I mean, everything's expensive in London, isn't it?"

"We get other money," I explained. "We get money from the police, from Mum's pension. And Jonathan gets some from social services, cause he's a foster dad. And *anyway*, even with the extra money, we don't have enough. There's loads of stuff Jonathan can't afford, like proper birthday presents."

"You don't get proper birthday presents?" said Kate.

"They do," said Jonathan. He looked even more embarrassed than before.

We did get proper birthday presents last year, because Jonathan spent some of Mum's savings on them. But that money's gone now.

Davy's birthday isn't until September, but he's already excited about it. He wants a bike.

"Not an expensive bike. Not, like, a super-fast bike with turbochargers or anything. Just an ordinary bike! Without lights, or brakes even."

"You need brakes," I told him.

But I don't think he was listening.

"They get birthday presents," said Jonathan firmly. He changed the subject.

You know how sometimes there are people you've known all your life, but you've never talked to them about anything more important than what boys you fancy or what bands you like? And then there are other people you've only just met, but you find yourself talking to them about things you've never shared with anyone else?

That's what Kate was like. After birthday presents, we moved onto parents, and Uncle Evan, and how useless Jonathan's dad is, and how we never see him, and Kate told us about her dad "who's *there* – I mean, he pays the bills and buys me Christmas presents, but I don't think I've ever had a proper conversation with him about anything that really mattered to me."

And Jonathan said, "I know. I worry that I'm going to turn into that sort of dad to Davy. It takes so much brain dealing with the day-to-day stuff like homework and shopping, I just don't have enough *space* left to think about anything else."

I thought Kate would say, "No, you won't!" or "I bet

you're a great dad really!" But instead she went off on a long tangent about how hard it was not to turn into your parents, and how you always noticed the faults in other people that you had in yourself.

"But it works the other way around too!" she said. "You notice the things other people are good at that you're good at too. Like – what was your mum best at?"

Jonathan thought. "She was funny," he said. "She told good stories. And she was always there – you could rely on her not to run away, like my dad did."

"Well, there you go!" said Kate, beaming at him.

In the end, I started falling asleep too, so Kate let me go to bed in her room instead of the living room. Kate's room had a high ceiling and an old-fashioned fireplace. There was mould growing on the wall, and a place where it looked like someone had kicked a hole in the plaster. (Kate kept old wine bottles with candles stuck in the top of them in the hole.) The walls were covered in tour posters of bands I'd never heard of, and student plays, and protest marches, and photographs of Kate and her friends in pubs and on muddy walks halfway up mountains and dressed in silly costumes. I recognized Katniss Everdeen, Buffy the Vampire Slayer and Hermione Granger. She looked pretty happy in most of the pictures. I wondered if Jonathan would have been living in a room like this if he'd gone to university instead of looking after us. Probably not. Jonathan wasn't as cool as Kate. But still.

I was pretty tired, but I lay awake for a while, listening to Kate and Jonathan talking in the living room.

I think they were trying to be quiet, but every so often I could hear Kate's delighted laugh. Once or twice I heard Jonathan laughing too.

I fell asleep listening to their voices in the next room, thinking how lovely it was going to be going on an adventure, how nice it was to have somewhere to be going to, and how wonderful that people were so kind.

When I woke up a few hours later, I could still hear them laughing.

CARRIED SLEEPING
ACROSS A FRONTIER

When I next opened my eyes, it was morning. I was in Kate's bed. Warm summer light was coming through the windows. It was going to be a nice day.

I lay there for a while, enjoying the laziness of it. Then I got up and went into Davy's room. Davy was sitting on the bed in his pyjamas playing with his Lego Millennium Falcon.

"Where's Jonathan?" I said. "Is anyone else up?"

Davy shrugged. "I've been playing," he said. "Do you think Kate has any breakfast?"

We went and knocked on the living-room door. There was a grumbling sort of noise from inside, then Kate's voice saying sleepily, "Come in . . ." We opened the door. Kate and Jonathan were lying on the sofa, which had been made into a bed. Kate was wearing green pyjamas with cats on them, and Jonathan was wearing a T-shirt that said RESISTANCE IS FUTILE.

"What are you doing?" I said. "Jonathan! Why are you in bed together?"

"Holly. . ." said Jonathan.

Kate pushed her red hair out of her eyes and gave a huge yawn. "Is this how they usually wake you up?" she said. "We were sleeping! It got late and we didn't want to wake you up! Honestly!"

"Hmm," I said. "Is there breakfast? Can we eat it?"

"Probably," said Kate. "Do I have to get up right this very second? If you make me and Jonathan a cup of tea, I might be persuaded to make you pancakes."

"I will!" yelled Davy. He ran into the kitchen to fill the kettle.

Jonathan gave Kate an impressed look. "Tea in bed," he said. "You are an evil genius."

"I have my moments," said Kate. "And I've had another one. I think I should come with you. No – don't argue," she said, as Jonathan opened his mouth. "Let me finish. I've been to Orkney. It's great, but it's less great if you don't have a car. You have to spend ages waiting for buses, and looking for bus stops, and lugging Scrabble sets around while you try and find the ferry port. It'll be much easier and quicker if I'm there. I've got a tent. And I'd love to come. Treasure-hunting! I've never been on a treasure hunt."

"Are you sure?" said Jonathan. "I don't know . . . you've been so good to us already . . ." He hesitated.

I could see him wanting and wanting to say yes, but not wanting to ruin it.

"Of course you should come," I said. "And Jonathan thinks so too. He's just too cowardly to say so."

The ferry didn't leave Aberdeen until late afternoon. Jonathan and I had planned things to do in Aberdeen that didn't cost any money, in case Kate didn't want us to hang around her flat – this hadn't taken very long, because there wasn't much. Mostly, there was a park and some museums and an art gallery and a library.

Now we'd met Kate and Kate had met us, though, things were different. We had a lovely day. Kate made pancakes, which we ate with bananas and Nutella, and tasted totally amazing. Then we watched *Ferris Bueller's Day Off*, because we'd never seen it and Kate said it was one of her favourite films.

"Now I feel a failure," said Jonathan, when we'd finished. "We shouldn't be in here watching telly. We ought to be off looking at art and dancing in carnivals."

"Wait 'til we get to Orkney," said Kate. "Ferris Bueller would have loved Orkney."

After we'd watched the film, Jonathan made mashed-potato surprise, which is mashed potato with whatever's left in the fridge mashed into it, and we spent the afternoon playing a silly card game where you had to fight monsters, which Davy turned out to be very good at. Then he went off to play with his Lego, and Kate

163

taught us how to play another game where you had to build roads and castles, and invade each other's cities. It was the most fun I'd had in ages.

And then it was time to go.

Kate's car was little and bright orange. There was a handle on both doors that you used to wind down the windows – except one window was taped shut with gaffer tape and didn't wind.

"It's called the Satsuma," said Kate. "Respect the Satsuma."

The ferry was enormous. Big enough to take us to France, or maybe even around the world. We had to drive the car into a great car deck at the bottom, like the belly of a mechanical whale. We parked, and then ran up to stand on the deck and wave goodbye to Scotland.

"Goodbye, Scotland!" Davy called. "Goodbye, goodbye, goodbye!"

Then we went inside and explored. There was a cinema, and a shop, and a bar, and a cafeteria, and a kids' play area with Viking helmets, and a treasure hunt with Vikings hidden all over the ship. Then we found a table, and Kate bought everyone hot chocolate.

"Please don't buy us things," said Jonathan.

"You can pay me back when you're millionaires," said Kate cheerfully. "Seriously, I consider this trip an investment in your treasure-hunting business. I expect ten per cent of the profits."

"There might not *be* any profits," said Jonathan.

"What would you spend them on if there were?" said Kate.

"A castle!" said Davy. "With – with – with towers that shoot lasers – powpowpowpow! And a water slide! And a spaceship – an X-Wing! And a dragon."

"Books," I said. "Lots and lots of books! I'd just go into Waterstones with a big bag and load it up with books. And new clothes. And make-up, like the rest of the girls have, and party clothes so I can go to parties and not look stupid. And a guitar. And—"

"A childminder," said Jonathan. "And university."

"You know," said Kate, "I bet university wouldn't cost you that much. You don't have to pay tuition fees if you're poor. And you could get a student loan."

"I couldn't rent a two-bedroom flat in London on a student loan," said Jonathan. "Even with the foster-care money, I couldn't. Or buy all the stuff those two need. I mean, do you know how much castles that shoot lasers *cost*?"

"I suppose so. . ." said Kate. "But there are places in London you can do part-time degrees. My aunt did one, *and* she's a single mum. They have all the lectures in the evenings. Maybe when Davy's a bit older, you could do one of those."

"I'd never sleep ever again!" said Jonathan. But I could tell he was a bit interested. I could see him thinking about it as the ferry chugged on north, and north, and north.

The journey to Orkney took for ever. At first it was

afternoon, then it was evening, then the sun set all pale orangey pink over the ocean, and it was night. We ate cheese sandwiches and Penguin biscuits. We played Spoons and Shop Snap and Uno and I-Spy and I'm a Famous Person, Who Am I? and Twenty Questions and Ghost. In the end, Davy fell asleep, curled in a ball with his head on Jonathan's lap. We had to wake him up so he could go to the loo and clean his teeth before we got to Orkney and had to sleep in a field.

It was weird, sitting there in this false, bright, manufactured room, floating on a sea of darkness. We could be going anywhere, I thought. Perhaps we'd land and we'd be in another world.

"Carried sleeping across the frontier," said Kate, when I told her this.

"Huh?"

"C. S. Lewis. The guy who wrote the Narnia books. It's how he described being converted to Christianity. But it always made me think of this bit in *The Odyssey* – do you know *The Odyssey*?"

"Er, no," I said. "I'm twelve."

"OK," said Kate. "Well, I read it at university. It's great. Mad, but great. Odysseus spends the whole poem trying to get back to Ithaca, which is the island he comes from. And at the end he gets a lift back from these sailors, and he falls asleep on the boat. And they don't want to wake him up, so they just dump him on the beach and leave him there. And when he wakes up he doesn't know where he is, because he's been away for twenty years. But he's home all the same. Kinda cool."

I smiled. "Yeah," I said. "Kinda cool."

It was really late when we landed. Jonathan's plans for this part of the trip had always been a bit vague. We had our tent, from when we used to go on camping holidays with Mum, but we didn't know where we were going to put it up. We'd vaguely thought that Orkney was all grass and fields, so there must be somewhere, right? But now we were here, it didn't look like fields. It looked like a little port town, with boats in the harbour, and houses, and concrete piers, and all the cars driving off down streets like they knew where they were going. It also looked dark. It was a long time since I'd put up a tent, and even then I'd mostly just done what Mum told me to do. I wasn't at all sure I'd know what to do.

Having a car made all that much easier. And Kate seemed to know a bit where she was going – she knew how to get out of Kirkwall, which was the main town, anyway. We parked in a lay-by and pitched the tents in a field. And she knew how to put up a tent – which meant that Jonathan had someone to help him. I just had to stand up and point the torch app on Jonathan's phone where they told me to point it. It still took ages, though. And was horribly, hideously dark. And then once the tents were up, we still had to put in all the tent pegs.

"I don't want to put in tent pegs," said Davy. "I want to go to sleep!"

He was ever so whiny, which is unusual for Davy.

Usually he's really good, but this was his second late night in a row, and he was nearly in tears, he was so tired. I wondered if maybe we ought to have left him with Gran and Grandad. They aren't really supposed to have overnight guests in their home, but I suppose it would have been OK just for a couple of days.

Once we were inside the tent, it was better. The tent was quite big. It had a place where you're supposed to put tables and chairs and stuff, and then two little bedrooms at the back, with an extra layer of tent to keep you warmer. I had one room and Jonathan and Davy had the other.

"This is OK, isn't it, Davy?" I said. It was OK. We had sleeping bags, and yoga mats, and a torch shining through the wall of the tent, making everything look orange.

"Be quiet!" said Davy. "I'm going to sleep now!" And he did. I'd been expecting it to take a while to get to sleep, because after all I was lying on a yoga mat on the ground in a field in Scotland. But I was so tired that I'd barely had time to think this thought before I was gone.

I woke once in the night, and heard the rain pattering down on the tent roof. An owl hooted somewhere. *Carried sleeping across a frontier*, I thought, and drifted back into sleep.

A BED FOR THE NIGHT

We got up early the next day, before a farmer could come and find us camped in his field. In the daylight, everything looked different. A clear new day, left wet and rinsed and sparkling by the rain, newly painted that morning on a big sheet of paper, with nothing ruined yet. The air felt light and cold and fresh. It smelt of salt and grass and mud and rain.

"Come on," said Kate. "Let's have a look around. The ferry doesn't leave for hours yet. Let's go and look at some of the old stuff!"

We drove around for a bit, enjoying the clear, bright morning. The island was mostly flat. There were hardly any trees – just patchwork fields in yellow and green and brown, and walls, and little roads, and behind us the low, long line of the hills. Here and there among the fields you could see little grey or white houses, sprouting up like strange Orkney mushrooms. Hardly anyone else was up yet, it was so early.

"Look!" said Kate. And there was a huge great ring of stones, each one two or three times as tall as a person, standing alone and eerie in the early morning light.

"What *are* they?" said Davy.

"Standing stones," said Kate. "They're thousands and thousands of years old. The people who put those stones up were old when the Romans came."

"Why did they?" he said.

But Kate didn't know. "No one knows," she said. "Isn't that cool?"

None of Jonathan's London friends thinks it's cool not to know things. They like facts, and data, and answers. But I thought Kate was right. Not knowing *was* a little bit exciting.

"All stone is old," Jonathan said. He was grumpy because he hadn't had coffee yet.

Kate laughed. "I can't decide if that's really deep or really stupid," she said.

The little town where the ferries left from was called Kirkwall. It was the biggest town in Orkney, but still small. Like, even the biggest street of shops was about half as long as the street of shops where we live in London. The town was just a huddle of low houses clustered around the harbour. And even the harbour was tiny. There were fishing boats, and yachts, and a jetty where our ferry would leave from, and not much else.

"What do you mean, not much else?" said Kate, like I was insulting her personal island. "Look! There's a cathedral! A pink cathedral! Right there!"

We studied Kate's cathedral thoughtfully.

"It's not *very* pink," I said. "More sort of pinkish brown."

"I thought cathedrals were supposed to be bigger than that," said Davy.

"They are," said Jonathan. "Come and have a look at St Pauls, woman. That's a proper cathedral."

"Yeah," said Kate. "But does London have an Orkney Wireless Museum? *I think not.*"

We found somewhere to park Kate's car, and then sat in a row on the edge of the harbour and ate chocolate-spread sandwiches for breakfast. The harbour smelt of petrol and sea salt. There was a wind blowing off the sea which flung my hair up into my face and made me glad we'd brought cagoules. It had been summer in London when we'd left – bare-legged, sunhat weather. Here it was sunny, but cold.

While we waited, I called Gran's friends on Papa Westray.

A lady with a strong Scottish accent answered. "I wondered when I'd be hearing from you," she said. "You're getting the nine-twenty ferry, are you?"

"Yes," I said. The nine-twenty ferry only took us to the next island, Westray. "Um. There didn't seem to be another ferry to you on a Sunday. But Gran said—"

"Oh, you can come across in the minister's boat," the

lady said. "We'll come over and meet you. I'll tell the boat to wait."

The minister's boat!

"OK," I said. "And – um – our friend Kate is coming as well. I'm sorry. I know we probably ought to have told you."

"Oh, well," said the lady. "As long as she's happy to sleep on the floor, it's no odds to me."

We went to have a look at the cathedral, but it was shut. When we came back, there was a little huddle of people waiting for a ferry. They were all dressed in cagoules and fleeces and woolly jumpers and hats, even though it was supposed to be July. Other than that they looked like ordinary, middle-aged grown-ups.

"Do you think they're tourists?" I whispered to Jonathan. "Or do they live here?"

"Those two are engineers," said Jonathan, pointing. "Look. It says so on the back of their boiler suits."

"I think they live here," said Davy. "And – and – they come to Kirkwall to do their shopping."

The next ferry was much smaller than the one from Aberdeen. It had a blue nose, which opened up to let the cars on.

Davy was delighted. "It's a shark boat!" he said. "It's got jaws! It's going to eat us!"

It took about five minutes to explore the ferry. There was a narrow car deck, a Passenger Saloon, which was a grand name for a square little room with fake-wood walls, and old-fashioned brown seats. There was a cafeteria in the very bottom of the boat. There was a map of the Orkney Islands on the wall, and Davy and I spent ten minutes reading all the names out loud to each other. *Notster, Quoyburray, Keelylang Hill, Point o' the Scurroes, The Ool, Sneuk Head, Hill of Miffia, Tongue of Gangsta, Mucklegersty, Suckquoy.*

"It's like somewhere in a story!" I said.

"Everywhere's somewhere in a story," said Kate, which was almost the same as what Jonathan had said about stones. But I knew what I meant.

We ended up on the Passenger Deck, which was basically an outdoor corridor with benches on it. It was sunny, but windy. The sky was pale blue and full of puffy white-and-grey clouds. We stood and looked out as the ferry chugged past alongside the island. Orkney mostly seemed to be empty and made of fields and low, bumpy up-and-down hills in green and purple and yellow and brown. There were sheep in the fields, and little houses nestled in the folds of the hills. The sea was a dark navy blue and always moving, all the time, in busy little wavelets. Below the sun, it sparkled, a great patch of white light, and round the edges of the sun stain, the tips of the waves glittered and danced with light. The whole ocean looked happy to be alive.

It took about an hour and a half to get to Westray. It looked just like Orkney did, only greener and flatter and, if anything, more empty. The further we got from London, the emptier and more end-of-the-world-y things became. Soon there would be just bare rocks and sea and woolly mammoths.

"Welcome," said Kate, as the ferry chugged up to the dock, "to the Sands of Woo."

"Seriously?" I said.

Kate showed me her phone. *Sands of Woo*.

"Woo!" said Jonathan.

Gran's friends Derek and Shirley were waiting for us on the jetty. Derek waved when he saw us land. "Shall we go?" he said. "Our boat leaves from the other side of the island, but they said they'd wait."

Derek and Shirley were both old, but not massively so. Wrinkly but not decrepit. They lived on the actual island where Auntie Irene had hidden the treasure, which was tiny. It didn't have a proper ferry on Sundays, just the boat that took the minister across – he'd already done one sermon on Westray that morning, and now he was going to Papa Westray to do one that afternoon. This boat didn't have a car deck – Shirley had had to borrow a car from a friend on Westray to take us across the island and anyway, the jetty on Papa Westray wasn't designed for cars. If you wanted to bring your car to Papa Westray, you had to take it across on the big weekday ferry, and have it winched ashore by a crane.

It was rather wonderful, going across in the little boat. The wind blew my hair back against my cheeks and into my face. The boat went up and down, and the waves slapped against the side with an *achuu, achuu, achuu* noise.

"Look!" said the man driving the boat. "Do you see

that there? Dolphins."

"Dolphins!" said Davy. "They're my favourite thing!"

He looked astonished, and delighted, like the dolphins had been put in the water by the universe for the sole purpose of making him happy. Perhaps they had.

Papa Westray, the little island, looked exactly like an island in a storybook. The sort the Swallows and Amazons would camp on, or George Kirrin would own, or pirates would bury their treasure on, and then go to fight in other wars and leave it there to be discovered.

It sat low and rocky and green in the navy-dark sea. There were cliffs, and a beach, and a few small buildings and houses, and further in the distance, sheep in grassy fields. The water around the shore was turquoise, and the sand of the beach was pale cream. There were little birds hopping on the stones and fluttering around the bay, and honestly, if this wasn't heaven, I didn't think it could really be far from it.

Derek and Shirley lived in a stone house near the middle of the island. Jonathan showed Shirley his print-out map with the place where Auntie Irene had taken her photograph marked. It wasn't far from their house. Nowhere was very far from their house. It was a very small island. Three and a half miles square. For such a small place, though, it seemed to have a lot of things on it. A school, a youth hostel, a shop, a guest house, several churches, a nature reserve and a museum.

"It's about twenty minutes' walk away," said Shirley. "You can go after lunch."

Lunch was delicious – crabs caught that morning by fishermen on Westray. Derek and Shirley listened politely while I told them all about Auntie Irene and our quest. They knew a bit about it from talking to Gran, but not the details. They didn't get all excited about it, like Kate and Sizwe did, which I sort of liked. They were more like, *Oh, OK, that's a totally reasonable way to get some money*, which was more like how the people at the Maker Space had reacted. I thought Shirley and Derek would probably like the Maker Space.

The plan was to stay the night with them, and then get a sleeper train back to London the next evening. That evening someone on the island was having a sixtieth-birthday party, and apparently everyone on the island was invited, which Shirley and Derek said totally included us.

"We can celebrate finding the treasure!" I said. I waited for Jonathan to tell me there wasn't going to be any treasure. But he just carried on eating his crab.

We set out for the beach after lunch. The island was green and brown and mostly divided into little fields – some with neat grass and animals grazing, some all wild and unkempt, with weeds and old farm equipment and tangle. There were sheep, and cows (but not Highland cows, ordinary ones), drystone walls all heavy with lichen, and country lanes. It was very windy – the wind kept blowing my hair into my eyes. Jonathan carried the metal detector, and Kate walked beside him. I walked with a bounce and a hop and a skip. Davy pottered about at the side of the road – running ahead to see what was around the next bend, lingering to peer at the flowers in the ditches. He sang to himself as he ran about, one of Mum's happy songs:

> *K-K-K-K-K-Katy,*
> *B-B-Beautiful Katy.*
> *You're the only g-g-g-girl that I adore.*
> *When the m-m-m-moon shines,*
> *Over the cowshed,*
> *I'll be waiting at the d-d-d-dairy door.*

Songs. They're another thing that went when Mum died. Jonathan doesn't sing any more. *Well, why not?* I thought, and I started singing too:

> *O, when the saints go marching in,*
> *O, when the saints. . .*

To my surprise, when I finished the verse, Jonathan joined in:

> *Swing low, sweet chariot,*
> *Coming for to carry me home. . .*

"*Swing low . . .*" sang Kate, and Davy waved his bit of stick about to conduct us.
A band of angels, coming after me,

Coming for to carry me home.

This train is bound for glory. . .

A cow, poking its head over the wall, watched us with a placid expression, like nothing we could do would ever surprise it. I blew it a kiss.

And then we were standing on the grass, looking down on the beach.

"Is this it?" said Kate.

"I guess so," said Jonathan.

We looked at the photograph in the album. Then we looked at the beach again. It was hard to be sure.

"Well," said Kate. "At least it's not definitely wrong. Does that thing work?"

So then Davy and I showed her how to work the metal detector, and she detected her belt buckle, and her house keys.

"Where shall we look?" I said. "It could be anywhere!"

"It couldn't," said Jonathan. "It won't be under those rocks, will it?" He was right. The rocks looked like they went down all the way to the bottom of the sea. "So let's start with the bit that's in the photograph, and move out if we have to."

So we did.

We let Davy work the metal detector. He moved it all along the grass, and then back. A couple of times it started beeping, and we all got excited, but the first time we just found a fifty-pence piece and the second time we found a bent spoon.

Then we moved further out. Into the longer, tussocky grass. We moved the detector all through the grass, getting further and further out. We found a lump of rock with veins of iron running through it. We found a beer can, and a rusty-looking piece of railing.

We went back and forth, all the way through the field, and then back to the bit of beach in the photograph for a second time, in case we'd maybe missed a spot by accident. Then we went to the next beach along, and the beach after that. We found a piece of wood with rusty nails in it, and a lump of concrete with the bottom of a fence post still wedged into it. We found a pound coin, and a penny, and a toy horse, and a key with a plastic fob, and something that looked like it might once have belonged to a handbag.

And then we were done. And the briefcase wasn't there.

DONE

"Perhaps you got the coordinates wrong," said Kate.

"Perhaps you ought to keep your nose out of things that aren't your business," said Jonathan.

Kate looked a bit surprised, and a bit hurt.

Jonathan rubbed his hand across his face. "Sorry," he said. "I'm just … well. Sorry."

"We didn't get them wrong," I said. "I checked them, and so did Jonathan, and so did Jen. It's supposed to be here. And it isn't."

Davy began to cry. Jonathan and I glanced at each other.

"Aw, Davy, don't," said Jonathan.

Kate bent down and put her arm around him.

"It's OK, sweetheart," she said. "Come on. Everything will be all right, I promise."

Davy made a messy, wet, mumbling noise, which sounded something like Sebastian-my-rabbit-rent-Irene-Mum. I knew how he felt. People saying everything will be all right when it obviously won't be is one of my worst things.

"Davy's right, Kate," I said. "I know you're trying to be helpful and everything, but it's not your rabbit. Or your brother who never has enough money to pay the rent."

"I know—" Kate began, but all of a sudden, I couldn't bear it. I started walking back across the field as fast as I could. *If I don't have to talk to anyone*, I thought, *I won't cry. I won't cry. I won't.*

HEARTH AND STONE

Kate caught up with me at the gate. "I'm sorry," she said. "I am, really. You're quite right, I should have a sign on my head that says WARNING: TRIES TOO HARD TO BE NICE, AND THEN SAYS STUPID THINGS."

"That's a bit long for a sign," I said, and the tears I wasn't crying only slightly blurred my voice.

"See?" said Kate. "Even my apologies don't make sense." She smiled at me hopefully. "Listen," she said. "I want to go and buy some postcards. Then I'd like to show you something. It's one of my favourite things in the whole world."

I half shrugged. I didn't want to go and see stuff. I wanted to go back to Derek and Shirley's and hide in my room and read about the end of the world. But I didn't want to seem ungrateful. Kate had been lovely, and when people are lovely, you have to let them go and see their favourite thing in the world, even if you'd rather not.

We went back to the little island shop, which was tacked onto the youth hostel. The shop sold food, and loads of other things, like wool, and cards with lifeboats on them, and books, and things that people on the island had made, like jewellery and socks. Kate bought postcards, and carrot cake, and I bought postcards for Gran and Grandad, and Jo, and Jen, and Sizwe, and Neema, and Keith.

Then we went back down the road, towards the ferry. There was a farm with red doors and a red wagon wheel against the wall and a sign saying MUSEUM. We went and had a poke around. The museum was in a barn, and was full of old-looking bits of stuff – milk churns, and old clothes, and a cup with a moustache-holder to stop your moustache falling into your tea. We looked around for a bit, then we went back out and down a track marked ANCIENT MONUMENT.

"What is it?" said Davy, but Kate wouldn't say.

"It's Stonehenge," said Jonathan. "The other one's just a fake. It's a three-million-year-old spaceship. It's the one true cross!"

What it was, was . . . well. . . There was a wire fence, and inside the fence there were what looked like two little houses, very neatly made of stone and joined by a small passage. Only, someone had forgotten to put on the roof, and the outside of the walls had been packed with earth, so the houses looked rather as though they'd been dug out of a hill. Each house had a low door with a stone on top – we had to duck down to get inside, even Davy.

But inside the house, it was nice. There were shelves, or possibly small seats built into the walls. You could sit in the wall and look out of the door at the sea, and hear the noise of the waves against the shore, and watch the little birds wheeling in the sky.

There was a tourist sign, like the ones you get in National Trust places. It read:

KNAP OF HOWAR
ORKNEY'S OLDEST KNOWN FARMSTEAD

The farmstead at Knap of Howar is one of the oldest standing buildings in northern Europe. Inhabited between 3600 BC and 3100 BC, it originally lay well back from the seashore in a grassy area behind the sand dunes. Changes in the sea level over the centuries have swept away the sand which had buried the ruins.

Although this is the oldest known settlement in Orkney, it was probably just one of a large number of single-family farms scattered across the Orkney landscape. The farmers grew crops of wheat and barley and raised cattle and sheep. Their diet was supplemented by fishing and gathering shellfish. In many respects their lifestyle was similar to that of most of Orkney's population until modern times.

Next to the words was a picture of a stone hut with a thatched roof, built on a beach, with an ancient family doing ancient-family things like waving arrows around and mending fishing nets, dressed in what looked like thoroughly inadequate clothes for a Scottish island. But perhaps it was warmer then.

"It's over five thousand years old," said Kate. She was grinning. "It's three thousand years older than Jesus! It's older than Homer! And the Romans! And everything in London! And it's right there!"

I tried to imagine what the people who'd lived here would have been like. Had there been kids? What did they wear? What did they do all day?

"Are we going to eat that cake?" said Kate.

The grass was soft and kind of springy. The cake was home-made carrot cake made by someone who lived on the island, and Jonathan had bought a big bottle of lemonade too. It did make me feel a bit better.

"You know what?" said Davy. "Everyone who lived in that house is dead."

There was a pause. Then we all started to laugh.

"What? What's so funny! They are!"

"Imagine if something you made was still here in five thousand years," said Kate.

Davy liked that idea. "I could make something and bury it somewhere where nobody would find it for years and years and years, I'd write *MADE BY DAVY KENNET* on it, and then in the future they'd dig it up and I'd be famous!"

I'm not so sure humans are going to exist in five thousand years. Surely by then we'll have used up all the oil and all the coal, and probably all the whales and dolphins, and we'll all have died of pollution, or starvation, or overheating, or all three, and the icebergs will melt, and this little house will be flooded over and gone, and there'll be nobody left to remember the people who lived there, and nobody left to remember Davy and Jonathan and Kate and me.

I said all this, and Kate said, "Maybe. Or maybe we'll find a way to solve our problems. Maybe you will. Maybe by then we'll be living on Alpha Centauri. Maybe they'll pack up this house and put it on the moon!"

Maybe. I dunno. I dunno what's going to happen to humanity. I don't even know what's going to happen to us.

I wondered what Mum would have said if she was here. If she was alive, we wouldn't be sitting in this little house in Orkney. Which would be sad, because Orkney was awesome, although my mum was even more awesome. If Mum *was* here, she'd be trying to cheer us up. She'd be reminding us that life is brief and our everyday problems are meaningless when compared with the great sweep of time, or something. Which is all very well, but our everyday problems *aren't* meaningless. Bad things don't stop being bad just because there are good things in the world too.

The carrot cake was good, though. And the house *was* brilliant. I wished we could stay here for ever and never go home. No, I didn't wish that. If we didn't go home there'd be no one to save Sebastian. Not that I exactly saw how we were going to save him now, but I wasn't quite ready to give up hope yet. Kennets don't give up on family members, ever, even if those family members are rabbits.

NOTHING

"It isn't there," I said.

We were back in Shirley and Derek's kitchen. There was a pot of tea, and ginger biscuits.

"I don't understand," I said. "The other photograph worked. The one with the railway siding. We took the metal detector to the place where the photograph was taken, and the treasure was right there! So why didn't it work this time?"

I expected Derek and Shirley to say something reassuring, like "Oh well, you did your best." But instead, they exchanged a glance.

"I wonder. . ." said Shirley, and then she stopped.

"You wonder what?" said Kate.

"Oh. . ." Shirley stood up, and began gathering together the empty mugs. "Nothing really. Just. . ."

"Just what?" I said.

"Oh. . ." Shirley shook her head. "I'm just thinking out loud, that's all. Don't mind me."

"Thinking out loud about what?" I said. "What's nothing? Is it something about Auntie Irene? Do you know where she hid the treasure?"

But Shirley only smiled and said, "Ask me no questions and I'll tell you no lies. More tea?"

SUPPER

There were ninety-three people who lived on Derek and Shirley's island. They all knew one another, and sixty-four of them turned up to the birthday dinner in the youth-hostel dining hall. Sixty-four people and us.

They were all different. Some of them were farmers. Some of them worked in the shop and the youth hostel. Some of them had lots of weird jobs all strung together, like Gran had said Derek and Shirley used to, like taxi-driver-and-barman-on-Saturdays-and-postman-and-binman. Some of them were fishermen. And some of them had ordinary jobs like designing websites, only they did it on an island instead of in an office. There was a primary school with six kids in it, which sounded like something out of a picture book. The secondary-school kids went to school on Westray, by boat. Imagine going to school by boat!

"I want to live here!" said Davy, waving his cracker around.

The youth hostel was little, but full of people. There was a hall with tables full of food. There were pictures on the wall of old-fashioned islanders standing beside ploughs pulled by cows, and a mobile shop pulled by horses, and rows of schoolchildren in old-fashioned clothes. There was a bar in the corner which was the pub. Everyone was very friendly and interested in us and what we thought about Orkney. Even Davy forgot to be shy and started telling them about Sebastian, and his school in London, and the ferry with the mouth like a shark.

At first, I just thought everyone was being friendly. I mean, Derek and Shirley had been coming anyway, hadn't they? But as the evening went on, I began to wonder if something else was going on too. When I went to the loo, I caught Shirley standing in the doorway, a plate of meringues forgotten under one arm, talking away to one of the farmers.

"Yes, about then. Do you remember? White-haired woman, very determined. Stayed with me. Yes. . ."

I stopped.

Shirley glanced up and saw me looking at her. "Hello, Holly!" she said. "You people doing all right, are you?"

"Fine, thanks," I said. Shirley and the farmer were looking at me with polite expectancy, so I had to carry on walking.

But later, when I was helping take the plates back to

the kitchen, I passed Derek talking to a couple of women.

"Yes, I thought that's what happened. They've come all the way from London, you see, so anything you can remember. . ."

After the food, they cleared the tables away to one side of the room. Three of the islanders brought out a guitar and an accordion and a fiddle, and started playing dance music. The dances were a very energetic sort of country dance – lots of swinging people around, and galloping up and down the room. It was hot and exhausting, but surprisingly good fun.

I went to find Kate, who was standing by the door, watching the musicians. "I think Derek and Shirley are up to something," I said.

"So do I," said Kate. "Shirley was having a dead intense conversation with that old lady over there. I think it's about your Auntie Irene."

"Me too," I said. "Do you think she was friendly with Derek and Shirley too, like Grandad was?"

The music started up. A man with a microphone shouted, "All right, people, find your partners!"

Davy ran up to me and yelled, "Dancing! We need to dance!" and started tugging on my hand.

"We should dance," Kate agreed. "Shall we?"

"Are you going to dance with Jonathan?" I asked.

She looked a bit embarrassed. "Does he dance?" she said.

"No," I said. "But I bet he would if you asked him."

"Holly!" said Davy. "Come on! They're going to start!"

I danced two dances with Davy, and one with Kate, and one with Derek, and one with a bloke called Conrad with white hair and a pointy beard like a faun. Then I stopped for a rest, and I saw Jonathan dancing with Kate. At first he looked very serious and concentrate-y, like he was worried he was going to do it wrong. But then the dance meant he had to spin her around, and he did, and she was laughing, and he was laughing too.

And then I realized I hadn't seen Jonathan laugh like that in ages. I'd got so used to him looking awkward and worried and embarrassed and sad, I'd sort of forgotten that a long time ago, he used to be funny and happy and silly. I remembered Jonathan who used to laugh and laugh at his favourite TV programmes, who dressed up as a Jedi for the library World Book Day when he was in sixth form and took it all dead seriously, staying in costume all day and challenging the year sevens to lightsabre fights. I was in primary school then, but the school posted videos to YouTube, so I knew what happened.

Watching Jonathan laughing with Kate, and then them both sticking on the dance floor for the next song, even though he didn't have to, like he actually wanted to . . . it made me ashamed. I know it's not really my job to look after Jonathan, but it is a bit, because looking after your family is part of what it means to be a grown-up, and I am a sort of almost-grown-up. And if that *is* my job, then I haven't been doing it well, if a happy Jonathan is someone I can barely even remember exists.

TREASURE

And then it was time to go.

"There's a boat at half past seven," said Jonathan, before we went to bed. "We should get that one. We're getting the sleeper train from Aberdeen – I don't want to miss it."

But Derek shook his head. "No, you shouldn't," he said. "There's something you need to do here first."

"But. . ." said Jonathan. "We can't. We need to get back to London. We've got a train booked and everything."

"Conrad's taking a boatload of sheep to Orkney mainland," said Derek. Conrad was the man I'd danced with last night. And the "mainland" meant the biggest Orkney island, the one we'd camped on that first night. "He'll give you a lift. You'll be in Aberdeen in time for the sleeper."

"But—?" said Jonathan. "I don't understand. What's

all this about?"

But Derek wouldn't say. "You'll see," he said.

Kate and I looked at each other. There was this little excited fairy creature dancing about inside my chest. *I knew it*, I thought. *I did!*

Derek and Shirley woke us up early for breakfast. It was porridge with salt in it, which tasted nicer than it sounds, but still kind of weird.

"Where are we going?" said Kate.

"I'll tell you in the car," said Derek.

Derek's car was a rusty old jeep. Not the expensive sort, but the sort that has seats and windows and battered metal frame and not much else. It bounced about on the bumps in the road, making Davy giggle. Kate sat in the front, and Jonathan, Davy and I piled into the back.

"The thing is," said Derek, as we drove out of the farmyard. It was just beginning to get light. The sky was pale peach and yellow around the horizon, and a clear, light, aching blue and white over the sea.

"Thing is," he said. "I expect you've been wondering why your auntie took her briefcase all the way up to Orkney to hide. It's not the easiest of places to get to, as you know, and she'd presumably want to pick it up again sometime, after all."

"I did wonder," said Jonathan. "It's not like she had a house here, or anything."

"No," said Derek. "But she had Shirley and me. We go back years, your grandad and I – we were at school together, you know – and Irene and I go back nearly as far. I always liked your Auntie Irene. Smart as they come – and bloody-minded with it."

"Are you saying you and Auntie Irene were friends?" I leant forward. "Did she used to come and visit you here?"

"That's exactly what I'm saying," said Derek. "She used to come and lecture every year at the university at Inverness – just for a couple of days, you know, and afterwards she'd come and see us. She'd stay on the farm, when we still had the farm, and help with the animals. We used to have a little dinghy that she used to take out and sail. Just her, never Evan or Jo. She said she liked the time alone, to think, and look at the world from a distance. We were always happy to have her. She was one of the most interesting people I ever met."

"She was, wasn't she?" said Jonathan, nodding away.

"So," said Derek. "About a year ago, she called and asked us if she could come and stay. Completely out of the blue – she'd stopped the lecturing by then. And when she got here, she was obviously upset. She kept talking a lot of nonsense about Evan and Jo – things I wouldn't care to repeat. She didn't seem herself at all."

"Jo thought she might have had a stroke no one knew about," Jonathan said. "The hospital thought so too."

"That wouldn't surprise me," said Derek. "But, anyway, she didn't seem exactly ill last year. Just . . . agitated. She kept disappearing off on her own, and going for walks around the island."

"She was looking for somewhere to hide the briefcase!"

I said, excitedly. "She did hide it here! Didn't she?"

"I'm almost sure she did," said Derek.

"But," said Kate, "we went to the place in the photograph. There wasn't anything there."

"I know," said Derek. "But I was thinking. That last year . . . she was awfully muddled in her head. And she was always taking photographs – she loved photography. What if she just put the wrong picture into the book? I can't quite picture her as the sort of storybook aunt who wants you to crack a code before she lets you inherit her money. No, I think she just meant the pictures as a visual reminder for herself. So what if the briefcase was hidden on a beach that looked a bit like that one, somewhere not too far from here?"

"Yeah!" I said. "Oh, Derek, you hero! Let's go and look at them all!"

"I don't think we need to," said Kate. "I think Derek knows where it is."

"Not exactly," said Derek. "Come and listen to this." He turned the jeep off onto a bumpy dirt track that led through the fields and into a farmyard.

A man in an old flannel shirt came out of the barn as we drove in, wiping his hands on his trousers. "Now then," he said. He had a dog with him, a shaggy black-and-white sheepdog collie, like something out of a picture book. "Yes, you can stroke her if you want. Rub her under the neck – she likes that. What? Oh, Jessie. Her name's Jessie. And I'm Liam. And you're Davy, aren't you? Ah, you see, I know all about you."

"People around here knew your aunt," said Derek. "Not well, but . . . I asked if any of them remembered seeing her when she came last year. I hope you don't mind, Holly, but I showed them that photograph of yours. She must have been going to a beach that looked a bit like that one, so I thought I'd ask. . ."

"I remember your Auntie Irene," said Liam. "She spent a whole morning out on the beach down from the house, December last year. Terrible cold day it was – I was out too, fixing a hole in one of my boundary walls. I don't think she saw me, but I saw her, digging away. I couldn't work out what she was doing. I was worried, because I thought she'd leave a big hole on the beach, and it might be dangerous. But when I went to have a look, she'd filled it all in, and there was nothing there but sand."

"That's it!" I said. I gave a little bounce of excitement. "Thank you! We need to go there *right now*!"

"Not so fast," said Derek.

"No," said Liam. "Because, you see, it sat there safe as houses until a couple of weeks ago, when a man came up from England looking for it. He said he was your Auntie Irene's husband. He had a photograph of a beach, and some pages that looked like they'd been ripped from a diary. I don't know what that was about."

"That was Uncle Evan!" I said. "He came up here and didn't tell us! What did you do? Did you give him the briefcase?"

"The briefcase wasn't mine to give," said Liam. "But

it's a free country. We have a right to roam here – you can't stop someone going for a walk on the shore. So, yeah, I showed him where her beach was. He didn't stay long. But when he went, he took the briefcase with him."

WHAT JONATHAN PROMISED

"Uncle Evan!" I said, on the boat back to Orkney mainland. "Uncle Evan! I'm going to kill him! I'm going to go round his house and blow him up! And then burgle our briefcase! And then shop him to the police!"

"No," said Jonathan.

"Yes!" I said. "That's our jewellery! It belongs to us! We can't let *him* have it!"

"We're not going to let him have it," said Jonathan. There was a curious intensity to his voice that I'd never heard before. Jonathan's usually so quiet and vague. But not now. It was like he'd been blurry before and now he'd come into focus. "We're not going to burgle his house. And we're not going to call the police. But Auntie Irene gave that jewellery to us. And we're going to get it back. I promise."

I glanced sideways at Kate and saw something in her face that made me wish I hadn't. Something in the way she looked at Jonathan. It wasn't quite pride, and it wasn't quite affection, and it wasn't quite admiration. I don't really know how someone looks at someone they're in love with, except in films. But it made me feel ashamed to be watching, like I was spying on something private. I looked quickly away, and hoped she hadn't seen me stare.

A FUNNY LITTLE BASIN YOU CAN
USE TO WASH YOUR FACE IN

And then we had to go home.

Kate drove us off the ferry and to the train station in Aberdeen. We said goodbye on the station platform.

"Let me know what happens," she said. "If the jewellery isn't in there and you need to get to Polynesia, call me. We'll work something out."

"We could hijack a pirate ship!" said Davy, and Kate grinned.

"We absolutely could," she said, and she gave him a hug.

"Are we ever going to see you again?" I said.

"Are you kidding?" she said. "Of course you are! Holly, my mum and dad live in Stoke Newington. That's practically next door to you guys. I'll be home for the summer holidays in a couple of days – I'll see you then."

"Really?" I said and she laughed.

"Really. Now, shoo. Go and find your cabin. I want to say goodbye to your brother. In *private*."

We didn't let them be private, though. We ran down the corridor to where they couldn't see us and pressed our faces up against the window. I thought maybe they were going to snog, but they didn't. She held his hands, though – both hands – and talked to him like what she was saying was which-wire-do-you-cut-to-defuse-the-bomb important. When she stopped talking, they hugged for ages, like couples do on telly when they've just survived something terrible, like the end of the world. That's what their hug was like. But then the guards started walking down the train shutting the doors, so Jonathan had to come on board.

"Is she your girlfriend now?" I said.

"No," he said. "Shut up."

"She's nice," I said. "We like her. If you wanted to be her boyfriend, we'd totally approve."

"Shut up now," said Jonathan. But he was grinning.

I ought to have been sad on the way home, because we hadn't found the treasure. But I felt weirdly . . . well, not exactly happy. Well, maybe happy. Content. And then, I'd never been on a sleeper train before, and it was exactly as cool as it sounds. Jonathan and Davy had a cabin, and I had a cabin that I shared with a Japanese lady whose name was Momoko, and had never been to Britain before. She'd been here for two weeks and so far she'd been to Edinburgh, and Skye, and London, and Oxford, and Stonehenge, and York Minster and Beatrix Potter's house in the Lake District. She was going home the next day, and you could tell she was sad about it. I thought how wonderful it was that she'd wanted to go to Britain, so she'd just got on a plane and done it, and how when I was grown-up I'd do that too, only I wouldn't go to Edinburgh and Oxford, I'd go to India, and Africa, and Nepal, and America, and that little island in Polynesia that Auntie Irene had loved so much that she'd buried a part of Jo's inheritance there. And I wouldn't go on a plane, because of the environment. I'd build a yacht and sail there.

The train was just how I'd imagined it would be. I didn't have my own bathroom, but I had a bunk bed, and a blanket, and a nice gentleman on the platform asked if we wanted tea or coffee in the morning. There was a first-class lounge, with a notice that said that non-first-class people could sit in it if it wasn't too busy, which it wasn't, so we went and played Uno on one of the tables, and pretended we were characters in *Murder on the Orient Express*. Well, I did. Davy just pretended to murder everyone in the carriage.

Afterwards, back in my cabin, I lay on my stomach and watched the Scottish darkness swishing by through the window, and thought about how big and exciting the world is, and how full of adventures, and mystery, and beauty, and how happy and lucky I was to be alive. *I am lucky*, I thought. And I fell asleep to the *clackety-clack*, *clackety-clack* of the train going over the joins in the track, like in one of those films where James Bond is fighting the bad guys on a train roof. *Life is an adventure*, the train seemed to be saying. *Life is an adventure, an adventure, an adventure.*

And I am an adventurous soul, I thought. And the thought that I could go anywhere, and do anything, and that I had all my life left to do it in made me so happy that I rolled over, closed my eyes, and went straight off to sleep, with Scotland rushing past the window beside me.

WHAT JO SAID

"Whatever you do," I said to Jonathan when we got home, "you can't do it without me and Davy. You can't!"

"No," said Jonathan. He still had that in-focus look about him. "Whatever we do, we're doing it together."

"What are we doing?" I asked.

"We're going to see Jo," said Jonathan.

We all went.

I'd never been to Jo's house before. It was an old-fashioned terrace like ours, but bigger, with a fancy bay window, and no chip shop on the ground floor. She looked dead surprised to see us.

"We need to talk to you," said Jonathan. "It's important."

She took us into her living room. It had a big soft sofa,

and a big TV, and lots of kids' toys all over the floor. Her little boys were building a train track all down the middle of the room, and watching *Peppa Pig*. Her husband waved at us from the kitchen, then went back to cooking something with rice and real vegetables in it. I did what I always do in houses like this, which is feel super super jealous, and slightly ashamed of our stuck-together-with-Sellotape family, and then ashamed for feeling ashamed of Jonathan, and then just sad that my mum isn't alive any more.

I'd been really worried about what Jonathan would say. I thought – knowing Jonathan – that he'd get scared, or embarrassed, or awkward, or shy, and just stutter at her. But he didn't. He didn't even sit down on the sofa. He stood there in the living-room doorway and crossed his arms and said: "Jo, your father has our jewellery."

"What?" Jo looked startled. "Jonathan, are you sure?"

"Absolutely," said Jonathan. And he told Jo what had happened in Orkney, in far fewer words than I would have used.

Jo sat down on the arm of a chair, and listened. Her face had a sort of closed look on it, tight and worried.

"And I don't know why he'd want it," said Jonathan. "I mean, he's loaded, isn't he? He inherited everything Auntie Irene left. So I don't see why he'd need our jewellery. But he has it. And you need to help us get it back. Otherwise I'm going to call the police, and I have a whole island full of witnesses who say he took it. Well, quite a lot, anyway. I'm serious, Jo."

"Of course you are," said Jo. "And – Jonathan, I'm really sorry. But Dad doesn't have much money – well, he didn't. Mum hid all of it in those briefcases. There's hardly anything in their joint account – Mum had most of it in savings, only we don't know where, or how much, or anything. I'm sure he wasn't trying to steal your jewellery. He'll have been trying to find Mum's paperwork. If what you say is true, and Mum moved the briefcases that were in Norfolk Island and Inspired Solutions, then that's an awful lot of paperwork that's missing, and that means an awful lot of money. And – you know – he has the money you guys found, but it takes money to run a business and keep paying a mortgage. That'll be what he was trying to do, I'm sure."

"Are you?" said Jonathan. "I'm not. I'm going to go and talk to him, and I want you to come with us. And can we go now? I think the sooner the safer, don't you? I don't want him to sell the jewellery, or anything like that."

Jo sat without speaking. I wondered if she was as unnerved by stern Jonathan as I was. Her face was still tight with worry. But she said quietly, "Of course I'll come, Jonathan. And of course we can go now. I'll drive. We'll go right away."

UNCLE EVAN'S HOUSE, AND WHAT WE FOUND THERE

We went to Uncle Evan's house. All of us.

"Davy could stay here, if you wanted," Jo said, a bit uncertainly.

"No!" said Davy.

"In our family," I said proudly, "we do things together."

"Do you?" said Jo. "Good for you."

Jo didn't bother to knock at Uncle Evan's door. I thought it was a bit odd at the time, but Jonathan said she was probably too angry. She unlocked the door with her own key and marched straight in. "Dad!" she called. "Dad!"

Uncle Evan came out of the sitting room. He stopped when he saw us all there. "What's the school trip in aid of?" he said, to Jo.

"Dad," said Jo. "I'm sorry about your money. But

you've got to let them have Mum's jewels. I expect you just hadn't got round to telling us you had them – had you?"

"I don't know what you're talking about," said Uncle Evan. "If these—"

"Listen," said Jonathan. "Shut up now before you say anything you regret. We know you went to Papa Westray and brought back the briefcase. We know that briefcase had the jewellery in it – at least, we're almost certain. And we're sorry you don't have all the money you were left, but we know how much money was in that briefcase we found in that railway siding, and really, you don't have much to worry about. I think it would be best for everyone if you gave us the jewellery now, don't you?"

"If you can't keep a civil tongue in your head. . ." Uncle Evan began, but Jo interrupted.

"Knock it off, Dad," she said. "This isn't one of your power games. It's theft, or fraud, or concealment of property, or something illegal, anyway."

"Yeah!" said Davy. "And we'll call the police on you!"

"And we've got witnesses!" I said. "A whole island full of 'em!"

"And I don't care if you are my uncle," said Jonathan, looking fiercer than I'd ever seen him look in my life. "I'll see you in jail before I let you hurt my family."

Uncle Evan looked partly angry and partly guilty and partly confounded, like a kid caught out in a lie. His face was reddish pink, and there was sweat beading on his forehead.

"Oh, I've got the blasted briefcase," he said. "But there's no law against that. I don't know what's in it. I haven't even opened it. I don't know how."

BREAKING AND ENTERING

Wednesday evening, we took the briefcase to the Maker Space. Everyone was there: Jen and Alex, Peter, Keith and Steve, Jo. Even Sizwe and his mum came. Even *Gran* came. "I want to see where my Christmas money goes," she said.

But really she just wanted to see what was inside the safe, like everyone else.

Steve opened the safe, while everyone watched and Gran said things like, "Goodness, aren't you clever? Could you teach me how to get into my flat when I lose my front-door keys?" And then looked really interested when Steve started telling her about the lock-picking classes.

Inside the safe was the jewellery.

Auntie Irene's jewellery was somewhat disappointing. I'd been imagining a heap of gold and jewels, like Smaug's

215

hoard in *The Hobbit* – glittery, shiny things, possibly made of diamonds, or emeralds, or rubies. Something a bit like the crown jewels. But instead, the case was full of lots of jewellery boxes: flat boxes, and square boxes, and old-looking leather boxes. And inside the boxes were dull rings and ugly necklaces. They did have jewels in them, but not the enormous stonking great glittering jewels I'd been hoping for.

"Are these valuable?" I asked Gran. "I thought they'd be . . . shinier."

"I don't know," said Gran. She was turning one of the brooches over in her hands. "But nothing Irene ever owned was second-rate."

"They're ugly," I said, taking the brooch from her.

She smiled. "Your Auntie Irene wore this brooch when she met President Eisenhower," she said. "So!"

Jonathan came over to where we were standing.

Gran put her arm around him. "Look at my clever grandchildren," she said. "Look what you did."

"Holly did it really," said Jonathan.

"And me!" said Davy.

"Well, I'm proud of all three of you," said Gran. She gave Jonathan a kiss. He looked startled. "But then, I already was, you know."

THE VIEW FROM NOW

Writing a book takes a lot of time. I suppose it's quicker if
writing books is your job, and you do nothing all day except
sit in your shed and make stuff up. But if you're thirteen, and
have to go to school, and do homework, and help look after
your little brother, it takes *ages*. I was twelve when we went
to Orkney, and thirteen when I started writing this story. I'm
nearly fourteen now, and everything is different.

We took Auntie Irene's jewellery to a jeweller who is
a friend of Alex's. He bought it for fifty thousand pounds.
Jonathan said I could keep a piece for myself, if I wanted.
(Neither of the boys wanted any of it.) Most of Auntie
Irene's jewellery was really old-fashioned and fussy, but
there was a ring I liked, with a dark red ruby in it.

"Do you think it was Auntie Irene's engagement
ring?" I asked Jo.

"No," she said. "I've got that. But I think Dad gave that one to Mum when they were first married. Do you like it?"

"Yeah." I said. Then, "Are you still mad at your dad?"

"Oh, well . . ." said Jo. She smiled at me. "I think he quite liked that I stood up to him, actually. That's what he liked in Mum, you know. That she fought back. He spontaneously offered to look after the boys for the weekend the other day, so it looks like I might have to forgive him."

Having fifty thousand pounds suddenly drop into our bank account made a big difference to life. So did Jonathan getting promoted to a proper foster-carer allowance, which happened about three months after we came back from Orkney. If I suddenly found myself with fifty thousand pounds, I'd want to spend it all on cool stuff, like Caribbean cruises, and new clothes, and a swimming pool in the back garden, and a real private island all of my own, for holidays. Jonathan put most of it into savings, which at the time I thought was rubbish, but I suppose was quite sensible really. We did buy Davy a bike, though, and a red bike helmet. And I got a new school coat, and a skirt and a sparkly top to wear to parties. And Jonathan got a dishwasher.

We also paid for Sebastian to have a proper operation. He's much better now. He still has to have injections, and he will for ages and ages, but he's his normal rabbit self again. Jonathan says that Davy is not allowed to have any more pets ever again, and if he does, he has to pay for their medical treatments by robbing banks. But I think he's joking. Probably. Or maybe it's just because Davy says he wants a tarantula for Christmas.

We used some of the money to pay for Davy to stay in after-school club until half past five, which means I now get loads of time all to myself to do whatever I want. Which was amazing at first, but then I found I sort of missed having Davy around a bit. So now I look after him every Monday and Friday, and Jonathan pays me babysitting money. And Davy started Cub Scouts, and I started guitar lessons, and Jonathan joined a Dungeons and Dragons group every Monday in a room over a pub.

We still see a lot of Kate. That summer after we found the treasure, when she came home for the holidays, she spent an awful lot of time at our flat, and she took Jonathan to Late Nights at the Science Museum, and he took her to the Maker Space and she came to the pub afterwards and had lightsabre fights with Alex and Jen. And on the way home, I saw her and Jonathan kissing.

And all the next year, they rang each other up a lot, and talked on the phone for ages, and giggled and giggled. And we all went over to her mum and dad's house for dinner on Christmas Eve, and played board games, and her parents treated Jonathan exactly as though raising your little brother and sister was the sort of thing nineteen year olds did all the time, which was what most people at the Maker Space do, but normal grown-ups do hardly ever. And Kate lent me a whole stack of books she thought I'd like – *Good Omens*, and *Jane Eyre*, and

On the Beach, and *The Innocence of Father Brown*, and *The Hitchhiker's Guide to the Galaxy*, because she said otherwise they'd just sit in her old bedroom unread. And we went camping in Scotland for a week in the Easter holidays, all three of us and Kate. And then this year, she moved back down to London and got a little room in a shared flat and a job working for a youth theatre, and we saw a lot more of her. I keep asking her to move in with Jonathan properly, but she won't.

"Not just yet," she says. "Don't I see enough of you already?" Which I suppose is true.

And somehow, it's like all the people in our life have noticed that maybe we need a bit more help, now and then. Keith keeps inviting Davy round to play with his kids, who have this mad model railway track all around their garden, which Davy loves. And Peter gave him about six shoe boxes full of Lego Technic that he had in his attic from when *he* was a kid, which made Davy go bright pink with joy. And Jo started inviting him along every time she took her little boys to the pantomime, or the London Eye, or the zoo. And when Jonathan gave me a clothing allowance, she took me out to spend it, and bought me chocolate gâteau in a café, just me and her. And for my thirteenth-birthday present she took me to see *A Midsummer Night's Dream* in Hyde Park, just me and Sizwe, which was amazing, and I understood nearly all of the words without anyone having to explain them, which I think means I'm practically a grown-up already.

And everything is mostly just the same as it always

was, but somehow everything is different as well. I still feel like we're climbing a mountain most days. But instead of trying to run up Everest, it's more like plodding up Helvellyn. Sometimes it's rainy, but sometimes the sun shines. And we've got packed lunches, and friends to keep us company, and occasionally something amazing happens, which makes it all worthwhile.

And the view's to die for.

ACKNOWLEDGEMENTS

Thanks to everyone in the Oxford Hackspace for answering my questions and suggesting interesting things for Holly to Make and Do. Thanks to Dan Taylor at Virgin Trains for going above and beyond the call of duty when answering helpline questions along the lines of "So how could someone get from London to Orkney without paying any money in a way that would be legal, and if it wasn't legal, how plausible would this illegal method be?" I didn't use your solution in the end, but your advice made sure the rail journeys in the book don't break the law and actually work.

Thanks to Stephen Barber for an incredibly useful afternoon explaining what happens at a review and what social services would and wouldn't be able to do for

Jonathan. Any social-service inadequacies in the book are entirely down to Plot Monkeys.

I made my first trip to the Orkney Islands with Nicola Bowerman and have been in love with them ever since. Thanks for taking me there. Also thanks to Tom Nicholls, Caro Humphries, Matt Piatkus and Nick Wedd for being so accommodating when asked "Can we go on holiday to Orkney? I'm writing a thing." Holly would have loved you all. Particular thanks to Tom Nicholls for talking me through how to hack into computers and find the location of buried treasure from photographs, and generally reminding me to leave the house occasionally. On these most useful of skills are great marriages made.

Much gratitude as ever to book-wranglers, typing-buddies, joy-cheerers and woe-sympathizers on and offline, particularly Susie Day, Pita Harris, Jo Cotterill, Tara Button, Lee Weatherly, Teri Terry and Cas Lester. Also thanks to my editors Gen Herr and Emily Lamm for their good sense and enthusiasm, and my agent Jodie Hodges for understanding the sort of author I want to be and allowing me to be it. And a grateful shout-out to the writers retreat at La Muse, Labastide Esparbairenque, where much editing and cheese-eating was achieved.

An Island of Our Own owes a great debt to Nevil Shute's *Trustee from the Toolroom*, which I read and loved when I was twelve years old, although the finished product bears little resemblance to it. I don't know what story Shute would have written if his characters had had the internet, but it would have been amazing. And would almost certainly have involved more aeroplanes.

Papa Westray is a real island, and Makerspaces (or Hackspaces) are a real thing. The people I've populated them with are entirely fictional, though.

Sally Nicholls was born in Stockton, just after midnight, in a thunderstorm. Her father died when she was two, and she and her brother were brought up by her mother. She has always loved reading, and spent most of her childhood trying to make real life work like it did in books.

After school, she worked in Japan for six months and travelled around Australia and New Zealand, then came back and did a degree in Philosophy and Literature at Warwick. In her third year, realizing with some panic that she now had to earn a living, she enrolled in a master's in Writing for Young People at Bath Spa. It was here that she wrote her first novel, *Ways to Live Forever*, which won the Waterstones Children's Book Prize in 2008, and many other awards, both in the UK and abroad. Her subsequent books, *Season of Secrets*, *All Fall Down* and *Close Your Pretty Eyes* have all been published to critical acclaim.

www.sallynicholls.com

LIST NO. 1 FIVE FACTS ABOUT ME

1. My name is Sam.

2. I am eleven years old.

3. I collect stories and fantastic facts.

4. I have leukaemia.

5. By the time you read this, I will probably be dead.

Every minute counts.